JOURNEYS

Journeys

Dorothy & Fran ~
May all your
journeys be
blessed & joyful!

Mary Jane Casey Lane
_2014_

Mary Jane Casey Lane

Library of Congress Control Number:		2014915019
ISBN:	Hardcover	978-1-4990-6467-4
	Softcover	978-1-4990-6469-8
	eBook	978-1-4990-6468-1

GNT
Scripture quotations marked GNT are taken from the Good News Translation
— Second Edition. Copyright © 1992 by *American Bible Society*. Used by
permission. All rights reserved.

Rev. date: 10/27/2014

To order additional copies of this book, contact:
Xlibris
1-888-795-4274
www.Xlibris.com
Orders@Xlibris.com
665699

CONTENTS

DEDICATION

For my brother, Joe

I Love You

AGONY MOMENT

A Short Story
By
Mary Jane Casey Lane

The army soldier who was standing
in front of the cross
Saw how Jesus had died.
"This man was really the Son of God." he said.[5]
Mark 15:39

CLETUS Friday Noon

With each step dust ballooned up his legs and then mushroomed as it descended and settled to the dirt that they had breathed, eaten and combed from their hair for wee ks. There was sand everywhere even on the city's cobbled streets. The heat, humidity and lack of rain only made matters worse. Dirt roads surrounded the city. There were few roads in and out of the city and those were in very poor condition, more sand discouraging travelers. However today the city is infested with hundreds and thousands of Jews, some from great distances, celebrating Feast of Tabernacle in Jerusalem's temple, one of three festivals held in the city each year.[3] Sand was an ever existing problem. So much so that when entering a home, poor or wealthy, you were asked to leave your sandals at the door. Many wealthy homeowners had slaves who would wash your feet before you actually entered and tread on their marble floors. Cletus had never been invited by the wealthy but he'd heard others tell about it. With holiday travelers added into the mix the city dwellers were not as cordial or hospitable, more irritable. The desert heat added more misery. Jerusalem· had not had rain for months so that even breathing seemed labored. Hopefully the black clouds and lightning slicing through the air a few miles to the West held the promise of relief. By the looks of the sky, dark and brooding, it was going to be a powerful storm. The strangest and most unsettling condition was the air. The color! It was yellow everywhere! It was as though a yellow fog invaded every breath they took, every destination they sought. Almost ethereal, enveloping the whole city. It was strange, layer upon layer tempting you to pull it aside as you would sheer window coverings, hoping to see the scene beyond it more clearly. You wanted to erase the film before your eyes. But pushing through only took you to another layer. Cletus stopped, looked around. The yellow presence was everywhere. The air was so dramatic, gritty and yellow! Ahead were the three ominous uprights, incomplete without the cross beams, soon to bear three bodies. The yellow haze made them look like they were swaying- optical trickery. Where had he seen this mirage before? Veils gliding through the air, enticing the observer? The costumes of the court dancers; sheer fabric enhancing their suggestive movements, provocative and seductive. A man could imagine pulling the gossamer aside and seeing the vision beneath; not possible for the ordinary man, however. In court it was just a mirage for insignificant guests like himself. Such privileges a reality enjoyed by the host and his illustrious guests. Cletus would not seek such a privilege even if it were offered him. He would not disrespect Claudia in that way. Claudia had stolen his heart the minute he first set eyes on her!

When he left the road to trudge up the hill there was an entirely different seduction taking place. To the Roman mob ascending the other side of the hill the seduction was the thrill of blood-letting and gore. The mob mentality much the same as school yard fighting; school children circled around two playmates on the ground and shouting, "Fight! Fight!" until an adult would drag them to their feet; the chanters running away. The sad difference was that those gathered here were encouraging, if not demanding; pain and suffering until death without any interruption. To these people death was the ultimate seduction.

Here were Roman citizens and others. "Crucify!! Crucify!!" And there was no one, not one person who had the courage to speak against what they were doing. No one was running away from this scenario. Where were his followers now? All in the mob were either in accord or too cowardly to speak out against the punishment. The crowds were 20-25 deep. Those in the back strained in an effort to see as much of the crucifixion as possible. Like Jack-in-the-boxes heads bobbed above the crowd only to disappear so quickly that under other circumstances might be humorous to watch. Cletus wondered at the insensitivity and loss of civility of the Roman people of today. Rome was supposed to be in its glory. Is there glory in hate? Is there glory in encouraging suffering and finding pleasure in abuse and pain? He shook his head in disgust, but his thoughts surprised and confused him. He looked away. What was the matter with him? For a soldier this was dangerous thinking. What was he doing thinking such thoughts? Loyalty was called for here. And why? Among his comrades such sentiments would be suspect. He was a Roman soldier, hard and obedient! Weakness was something a Roman soldier never exhibited. Cletus turned to the crowd again, hoping these unexpected feelings did not expose what would surely be suspicious, even betrayal, coming from a Roman soldier. To the Roman populace soldiers were to be feared. Not soft or intimidated. Compassion would label a soldier unfit for duty and probably not fit for much of anything else. Cletus would do anything to avoid that humiliation. Though his hands trembled, he recovered and stood ramrod straight, held his head high and his stance authoritative. Let Pilate worry about the people of Rome; let him worry about

Rome's image. He picked up his nails and mallet, ready to do his duty. These people were fools! Truth be told, today was craziness! Cletus noticed but was not surprised that the mob was being led by a group of priests from the temple. He was privy to court gossip and convinced that the priests did not come to the crucifixion to pray for the criminals. They wanted this man called The Christ out of the picture.[3] The Christ was a radical, questioning their interpretation of religious laws. It threatened their high standing in the temple. Cletus was not a religious man but he knew of the greed of these so-called temple elite. Especially Caiaphas, high priest, had much to lose if The Christ and his followers actually seized the temple and established The Christ as king. The title of high priest is carried for life and Caiaphas wanted to make it a long and comfortable one. Caiaphas' pockets were deep and he worked closely with Pilate. Talk among the military was that Caiaphas receives a cut of the exchanges made by the money changers in the temple. The high priests in general owned vast farms and estates, profitable ventures, as they received a share in the taxes gained in this way. Caiaphas owned a lavish estate outside the city. It was rumored that he also benefited from the taxes of the general citizenry.[3] Much income was generated as his percentage from the sale of slaughtered lambs required for sacrifices, a market that was not likely to dry up. Cletus wondered, "Is Caiaphas in Pilate's pocket or is Pilate in Caiaphas' pocket? Or just maybe they took turns carrying the same money bag?"

Today an overseer was assigned to make sure all went according to the law. Cletus noticed that the court physician was in attendance. Physicians are not required to be present unless called upon to determine death if there's not a certainty, especially if the body had been taken down. The crowd parted to allow him to the foot of the cross. A chair was provided for him; this could take several hours. He watched the scene before him. Things had better proceed legally because we were all sure he had Pilate's ear. Usually a squad was made up of only four soldiers. But the nervous Pilate has sent more soldiers to keep order. He knew this crowd could be unruly. His washing of hands was not honest symbolism. There is plenty of guilt to go around.

Cletus is nervous because of the direction his mind had taken him. Perhaps Cletus had never thought himself a man of principle. He couldn't understand it. He wanted this charade sealed and finished. He was not comfortable with the way things were panning out. During his introspection he missed all that had been going on. The Christ had already been placed on the crossbeam but not yet lifted to the vertical beam. His hands had already been nailed to the crossbeam; how could Cletus have possibly missed the screams of pain as the nails had been driven in? Cletus reverted to an emotion that men often do when they suffer guilt or disloyalty; he got angry.

The storm refusing to be up-staged, tried to rein in his anger as cloud collided with cloud, a dueling match, leaving those in the crowd startled as one would when a friend sneaked up behind and screamed, leaving you shaken, even though you knew it was a prank and you were perfectly safe. Cletus allowed his anger to merge with each cacophonous clap hoping for its demise. Perfect syncopation. Storm all around him and storm playing havoc with his mind, hand in hand. Cletus suffered as most do when they find they have a conscience, a new and bewildering synapse for his mind to assimilate; in this case, questioning motives. Yes anger would work, at least temporarily and Cletus allowed his anger to surface. Again this was supposed to be his day off. He wanted to spend some quality time with his eight-year-old son, Jonas. He had been pulled as a substitute. He was angry alright but was also concerned about Titus. He knew Titus, his best friend, was assigned to this squad in the same role, nailing of the feet. Titus is the one he'd been called to replace. What had happened? He was determined to either give Titus a piece of his mind or discover what mishap had befallen him. He would always be there for Titus and knew Titus would always reciprocate. But mostly he needed a scapegoat to satisfy his anger. A soldier on a ladder was climbing to the top of the eight foot vertical beam while two soldiers struggled to lift the crossbeam bearing The Christ's body up to the groove which had been cut out to accept the crossbeam. This would take a while.

Cletus slowly scanned the scene before him. The Christ was now hanging from the raised cross. His pain must be excruciating! The crowd looking up had already made room for each other. They were quieter, seemed nervous, overt gesturing as they spoke. Human nature often after the fact questioned the wisdom of their decisions before the fact. Demands to crucify had been satisfied.

Too late to change one's position regarding what was taking place here. The nervous energy in the air was almost suffocating! Cletus trembled and the trembling angered him even more. In an attempt to rein it in Cletus shook his head violently, hoping its eruptions, like a volcano, would spew forth his anxiety- thoughts he was certain would lead to his ruination. He had to redirect his anger; it was imperative that his thinking go to another place. Cletus turned to his "hands" soldier who serves with Titus on this squad. Maybe he would know what happened. "Where is Titus? Why isn't he here?" In reply the soldier shook his head and shrugged. "All I know is he was present at the scourging as required. Like the rest of us he was on duty through the night. And he was with the prisoner as he carried his cross; then suddenly he said he felt sick and hurried away, probably to the court physician. He seemed all right until we reached the summit."

This worried Cletus. Titus was like a brother to him. They shared everything. They shared their dreams for the future. If Titus did not have a very good reason for being absent he stood to be reprimanded; maybe even prison time. Cletus couldn't imagine that happening- but this was Rome. Soldiers were esteemed though they held no place in the hierarchy. They were soldiers respected for their bravery and often their cruelty. Barely a step up from common citizens.

He and Titus had met in squad training. As candidates for crucifixion squad they had both studied under the same court physician. Studies were intensive. They had to know bone structure of both the hand and the foot, knowing the exact place to drive the nail; the foot had to be flexed at an extreme angle so that suffering would be greater because the criminal would instinctively try to hoist his body up. This affected the lungs ultimately resulting in asphyxiation; the man would die of suffocation. The victim would push on his feet, trying to expand his lungs, actually causing him to suffer more.[3] Other cities in the empire often constructed a seat for their victims. However, the purpose was not to relieve but to cause a slower death. The length of time it would take to die by crucifixion could be hours to days depending on factors including environment. How the impending storm would play out for this incredibly strange man on the cross remained to be seen. The lightning flashed one after the other like strands of pearls on a long necklace. Thunder created such a din that it was impossible to carry on any conversation, making it feel as though you were all alone facing a destruction of unheard of dimensions. Fear turned away many in the crowd, like black specters fleeing in all directions. The yellow haze added evil to a now demented and frenzied scene. Those with courage stayed. Cletus noticed that the priests remained.

And almost like a miracle the storm quieted, and though still very threatening, was seen as yet a good distance from Golgatha. The court physician knew death was near. The Christ was struggling to stay erect. When he was unable to continue lifting his body death would come in a few moments.

Cletus turned his thoughts to Titus. They had studied together and were disappointed to be assigned to different squads. It was inevitable that they became like brothers. Cletus would trust him in any circumstance. They understood each other. They truly believed they were honoring Rome. Titus was a good soldier, loyal and obedient. He was a perfect role model for new recruits. He'd often been assigned to their training and he was respected by his superiors.

A sign for Cletus to begin interrupted his thoughts. He would get this over with and then decide what to do about Titus. Taking a deep breath, he thought, now the deed will be done. Sweat poured from his face as he arranged the feet to the perfect angle, placed the nail carefully and gave a powerful swing with the mallet so it would be done quickly. The Christ's head jerked backward, then forward, then down. The most blood curdling scream silenced all present. The silence was almost tangible! Almost painful. It was real! Cletus thought maybe the nailing had actually killed The Christ! Had his nail killed The Christ?! In his head all Cletus heard was his own voice, screaming "No-o-o-o!" The scream of agony from the cross was like a knife had plunged into Cletus' brain. He was stunned. He was certain he'd never be able to hold his head high again. Never had a crucifixion affected him in this way. He narrowed his eyes and looked up at The Christ. The agony moment was still on the face of The Christ and it was, for Cletus, as if the world stood still. He knew he had to make the next move. He had to finish this day! How had he dealt with this circus atmosphere? In anguish he cried, "The gods forgive me for inflicting such pain." He'd never prayed before and were there gods, he didn't know who they were. But he was desperate. Didn't these gods know he wasn't even supposed to be on duty this day? HE WASN'T SUPPOSED TO BE HERE!! He hung his head, sank to the ground, his hands covering his face, and tearfully whispered in anguish, "I wasn't supposed to be here." How long had the sharpened knife plummeted his brain? He had no idea. When in unforgiving pain, one lost count.

Again he was angry- sometimes it was his saving grace. But not today. He'd done numerous nailings before. Why should he care now? Why this man called The Christ? Why this man who was stupid to think anyone in his right mind would take him seriously? His followers were mostly simple inept peasants. They would revolt against the Roman Empire and win?! It's laughable! Who could believe him? Who would be threatened by a fool who didn't even try to defend himself? Oh, he was good! He had fooled many! Even Pilate was displaying unheard of caution. Did Pilate feel threatened? Thousands of well-trained soldiers against a handful of ignorant and simple followers? Impossible! Did this new anger make Cletus feel any better? Not really; but he'd tried. Of course he'd tried! After all he was a Roman soldier. He tried to stand a little taller. But hadn't he called all that had happened here today craziness? Not the thoughts of a soldier! A soldier could be disciplined for dishonoring Rome with such derogatory remarks. A soldier does not question, criticize or degrade the Roman government. Rome is never wrong and a soldier of Rome is honored to serve without question. Cletus' normal duty was as a prison guard, twelve hours daily from 10pm to 10am except when reporting for special duty, usually a crucifixion. Thankfully he was not on duty until tomorrow.

"Cletus, Cletus!" the hands soldier, trying to get his attention, yet not give him away, spoke in a stage whisper. Cletus lifted his head. "Stand up before someone notices. Stand at attention! You sat there for so long! The Christ is edging more quickly to his death. If you're not at attention when death is confirmed, you will pay the consequences. You know that! You take too many chances, Cletus! Stand up you fool!"

Cletus quickly assumed his posture, alert and observant. He might be called on to justify the duties and procedures taking place before him, especially considering the tension accompanying this crucifixion. All had to be legal in every detail.

Once again Cletus turned his eyes to the victim. He'd never seen such suffering and torment. The Christ's lips were moving as in conversation. His chest expanded and contracted. Exaggerated in need for air. Suddenly The Christ shouted out! Shouting that broke the silence. "What did he say?" Someone in the crowd translated that he had called out to his father. Another strange account. Victims usually called out for their mothers. The Christ's head dropped, slamming his chin to his chest. His jaws gaped open grotesquely, forming a silent scream. Following his last gasp for air his eyes remained open, glazed-over; with the vacant gloss seen only in death. The "death knell" tolled all the injustices inflicted upon this man, the would-be king. If Cletus had not tightened his muscles in shock he would have surely collapsed. His head pounded, "He is dead!" He has died and for what? A handful of friends; friends who did not even stand by him at death? Betrayal! He is innocent! Oh yes-s! Rome is much safer now. Rome is never wrong. After all he was just an unimportant, simple man who thought he was somebody we all know he wasn't.

And this poor man would soon be forgotten and all that had happened here would not go down in history. That was reserved only for important men. So we have to question why did we do what we did?

With all this said, Cletus had to accept he would be the only one in history, along with The Christ's followers, to place any special significance to these events. Cletus knew The Christ was innocent. And, oh, if only he could ignore the guilt he felt in his heart. What made him think this way; it boggled his mind? All he really needed was peace.

Suddenly the earth shook beneath their feet, threatening to open up and suck them into a dark and deadly abyss. Explosions rumbled through the city below the mob! Pandemonium! They wailed and thrashed about, attacking anyone in the way, positive that if they reached the bottom of Golgatha they would be safe. And incredibly the storm's destruction ended. The storm's journey from the West was slow and powerful. The tremors, so frightening, lasted only a minute or so. But all who had scattered from that infamous hill felt terror long after the tremors had subsided. The storm and earthquake would be remembered long after. None realized that what had taken place here today would impact all of history and all mankind to come. Picking up his tools he looked again toward the upright that was now missing the abused body of The Christ. At the foot of the upright beam stood a young man obviously grieving, trying to remain in control. Two women were standing beside another who was cradling the abused man known as The Christ. She was using her veil to clean the blood from his face. She had to be his mother; she looked as though she had suffered almost as The Christ. Something stirred in Cletus and he found himself striding toward the group, whose heads were lowered in sorrow. The sorrow. This is something he had not been trained for. Something intentionally omitted? A soldier was taught that Rome is always right, always strong! Until today Cletus had never considered sorrow. He cleared his throat and the woman tending The Christ looked up.

Quietly he asked, "Are you his mother?" She nodded then lowered her head again.

"I'm sorry." Now why had he said that? Why did he care how his mother felt? Her son was a very foolish man. Cletus needn't remain here. He would feel much better if he was sure no one had seen this interchange.

As he turned the young boy held out his hand as though to stop a trespasser. The young man, little more than a boy, turned so he could look Cletus in the eye. "Yes, this is His mother. Are you expected to inflict more pain on His family? Is it one of your assigned duties. You're the one who drove the nails into His feet, aren't you?" His voice trembled but he stood firm, his hands balled into fists. "Leave His family alone!" Cletus had to admire the boy for standing up to a Roman soldier, weapons clearly visible. Cletus merely offered a slight nod and turned away.

He stored his tools in the crib, a rough wooden box, unlocked. They had no reason to fear anyone stupid enough to steal soldiers' tools. He turned and walked slowly down to the dirt road by which he had come here. He headed toward home, bone-tired. Why didn't he feel good about himself? Why did he think less of himself? Damn it! Like it or not, this day was craziness from start to finish. And he'd never change his mind about that! He couldn't. Because deep in his heart it was real!

****

JONAS Friday 4 pm

There were so many people everywhere, especially along this back road. Many travelers on the road with him were pilgrims attending what the Jews called the Feast of Tabernacle. If they traveled this particular road they were, probably poor, hoping to stay with poor relatives.

Cletus paid them no mind; he was trying to erase the last three hours. He had a strong suspicion such thoughts would not stray far from his mind, his own special hell. He was just so confused about the way he was feeling! Those around him stared and wondered what a Roman soldier was doing in this part of the city. They pulled their children closer and gave him wide berth. Cletus too had to watch carefully. It was said, "A Roman was always subject to the gaze of fellow citizens." The nearest street was just ahead; he would turn there just as anxious to distance himself from their probing eyes. He hated these emotions! He wasn't accustomed to vulnerability and paranoia. He had to think.

However shouts of school children bounced off the walls and interrupted his thoughts. No school lessons? Of course, it was the close of mid-day- 11 am to 4 pm. At 11 am everyone headed to the Forum where they relaxed, free of responsibilities. Only "on foot" traffic was allowed on the streets, no "wheeled vehicles" so children could safely navigate the usually busy streets. Men, rich and poor alike, took advantage of the reprieve and went to the Forum to visit the baths. It was an expansive natatorium. The pool was massive, very inviting, especially in the heat that continued to punish Jerusalem. First a cold plunge into the pool invigorates and encourages conversation, the opportunity when the poor can talk to the men of influence and lobby for their causes. It had been at the pool that Cletus met a beggar, Eli, whose real career was the selling of information. The beggar persona a perfect cover for his illicit career. He had convinced Cletus to become his customer. A soldier with information of any import to Rome could win him many favors. Cletus suspected that Eli's information was often conjured up so he'd have to be very careful what and with whom he shared information gleaned in this way. "Quacks, soothsayers and charlatans of all shapes and sizes were around." A steam bath came next. A luxurious massage, oil spread over the entire body, likely the best part of the baths, followed. Outside children gathered in the playground where playtime imaginations would abound. Several children were running around while small groups of boys huddled close to the ground playing a game called Knucklebones. The bones of sheep or goats were commonly used. In one version of the game five bones were thrown like dice. The player tossed a stone into the air and tried to pick up all the bones, catching the air-born stone as well. The more experienced attempted to catch all on the back of their hand. As girls would be girls they sat in the shade of trees weaving necklaces and laurel wreaths to be worn in the hair. Girls did not attend school so they really looked forward to the play-time get-togethers where the other girls were waiting for their mothers to finish shopping as well. All the city shopped in the large farmers' market on the perimeter of the Forum. They purchased foods such as honey, beans, lettuce, cabbage, grapes; whatever was needed for the evening meal. Imported goods such as dates, apricots, citrus fruits and wine were popular with those who could afford them. Beer was seen fit only for barbarians, those living beyond the city limits. Mornings, boys on their way to school often stopped at the bakery located near the market for a pancake to eat on their race to beat the school bell. No meats were sold at the market. A variety of other shops were sprinkled around the Forum offering products from foreign markets, silk from

Mary Jane Casey Lane

China and shoes from Gaul. Shops selling local wares were crowded together as well.

Today the impending storm curtailed the much anticipated spa treatments or even just a visit to the Forum. Best to be at home when such a threatening storm growled all around them.

"Father! Father, wait up."

Cletus turned around and settled his gaze on the treasure of his life, his son, Jonas. "Father, you did not look for me at the playground like Mother said you would. She told me to wait for you there." Jonas was breathless. He hadn't run that far but he was frightened that his father had forgotten him. That had never happened before.

Cletus settled to his haunches, holding his arms out to capture his son. "Jonas, I was just thinking so hard. I'm sorry. Don't be frightened." He swung his son around in circles but didn't get the squeals he expected. He put Jonas down. He smiled down on him to reassure him, "Besides when I'd get to the shop where we stop every day to choose our favorite boat in the window and you weren't with me, I'd run right back to get you, excited to know which boat you'd choose today. There is no way I'd want to walk home without you. You do believe that, don't you?" Jonas looked like something more was bothering him, but answered, "Yes, I know."

30

Cletus, knowing something else was worrying his son, suggested, "I'm tired. Let's sit down and rest a little." They sat on the ground and Jonas picked up small stones and tossed them onto the dirt road across from where they sat. He kept his head down. "Tell me, Jonas. You know you can always talk to me, remember?" Cletus was no longer thinking of himself. He begged whatever gods there might be not to steer his mind to something else at the expense of his son.

Jonas turned and faced his father so they could look at each other as he told his story. "There were some boys at the playground talking about a man called Jesus. Do you know him?"

Cletus answered, "No." Next Jonas asked, "Did you nail today?" Cletus nodded yes. He wondered where this was going but he'd never heard of a man named Jesus.

"Some of the boys know the man you nailed. They said he is very kind and smiles and makes them laugh. They said he is a good man. They like him. His name is Jesus. They said today he was crussifried!" A small smile at his son's mispronunciation. Claudia and Cletus had never used that word in Jonas' presence. "And they said that you murdered him. They called you a murderer!"

This was a time for truth no matter how difficult. "Jonas, there was a crucifixion today. But it was not a man named Jesus. This man was called The Christ."

"Father, that's him! One boy said that some people called him that, but his real name is Jesus."

Cletus hung his head. He plucked one blade of grass after another and watched as the wind picked them up and blew them aloft in the air. Jonas' eyes filled with tears, stared at his father and at first Cletus could not look at his son. Tearfully, Jonas finally asked him, "Are you a murderer, Father? Those boys were shouting at me "murderer" so I ran to the street where I thought you would look for me! Please tell me you are not a murderer!"

Cletus could not live with his son thinking that of him. He was not a murderer. He was following orders. He stopped plucking and slapped his hands on his thighs as a signal to answer thoughtfully and confidently. He hoped he could. He looked into his son's eyes and let out a long slow breath; could emptying your lungs give you brand new breaths, confidence when you speak? Please!

"Jonas, I'm glad you talked to me about this. I think you are old enough to hear this. Those boys just don't understand what it means to be a Roman soldier. A good and strong soldier promises to protect all Romans rich or poor from anyone threatening harm to Rome. A promise is an important thing. Just think if someone gets really mad and wants to hurt you or your mother. What would you expect me to do?"

"Keep them away from us."

"Exactly. And I would, Jonas, I would! I would protect you from the enemy. And if I thought you were in danger I'd have to do something." How could he make a small boy understand?

"Would you kill them?"

"Not unless I had to because they were ready to hurt us and there was no one to help us.

"I couldn't just watch them hurt you or your mother. But that would not be murder, that would be protecting you or even myself. If I knew someone might hurt us I would have them arrested and a court would decide how to punish them. The Christ was found guilty of trying to overthrow the Romans and that he should die for wanting to bring harm to us. When a man is to be punished by crucifixion it is soldiers who do it. And that's exactly what a Roman soldier should do. We live in a very big empire, miles and miles all around us. We have to protect all our people. There has to be an army to fight for us if there is no other way. To be a soldier we must believe that Rome is glorious and rules the world. Roman soldiers must be hard and obey all they are told to do. What if some soldiers decided they would not do what they are told? There would be fewer soldiers to protect us from our enemies and our enemies might be stronger and might defeat us. To be a soldier in

Rome is an admirable thing. I am proud to be a soldier and I want to be a good one! Today I did what any good soldier would do; I obeyed orders. Jonas, I am not a murderer and I do follow orders even when I disagree." Was he trying to convince his son or perhaps himself? He could not allow Jonas to be ashamed of his father! So ...... he lied!

Cletus looked at Jonas and saw the pride reflected in his son's eyes. It broke his heart. Jonas smiled, "Then you are not a murderer because you saved us from The Christ. I guess sometimes it isn't easy to be a good soldier but I want to be a soldier just like you, Father. I will obey and follow orders. How old do I have to be to be a soldier?"

"It will be many years before you can be a soldier. In the meantime do not talk to those boys again. Promise?"

"I promise, Father." Jonas looked up at him with those bright green eyes, the color of sea waters. "And do you know why. Father? Because my father is a Roman soldier and I am going to be a soldier just like him when I grow up. And soldiers keep promises." Jonas shook his head up and down as though that gesture sealed it!

As Jonas slipped his hand into his father's hand Cletus felt several emotions and didn't understand most of them. "We'd better hurry. It's starting to rain harder. Hurry!" The storm just minutes ago changed from a hell-bent threat to the promise of reprieve from the heat and the arid ground beneath their feet. The yellow presence gave up its mystery, embracing the welcome of clouds as they began their work to wreak havoc another time and another place. The rather abrupt lifting of the yellow haze magnified the color spectrum left behind with a nearly blinding reward for all the days of yellow.

Both father and son had reason to dwell on new thoughts of differing direction. They did not stop at the toy shop.

Cletus had avoided the part of soldiering that usually demanded soldiers wage war. They never knew when that would come. They were expected to be on the ready. Claudia and Cletus were prepared to make that sacrifice. They were expected to satisfy Rome's passion for power.

Oh gods, what had Cletus done to cover up his guilt? For Cletus his heart was a target; little darts of guilt and shame punctured it again and again. How soon would there be nothing left of it? Then Cletus would truly be a heartless soldier! He allowed a sad smile at the pun he hadn't meant to create.

After Jonas had gone to bed Claudia touched her husband's arm. "Well this evening has been awfully quiet. Jonas came home elated. But his father looks like he carries the weight of the world on his shoulders." Cletus' eyes looked so troubled. She wanted her two men whom she loved very much to be content and happy. "What's wrong, Cletus?".

He placed his hand over hers still resting on his arm. He sighed. There was so little air in his chest to comfort him. "Claudia, come sit with me. I'll tell you about my day and Jonas' day.

****

TITUS Saturday morning

Cletus' heart was so heavily laden that he'd had trouble falling asleep.

Only to have a nightmare! Jonas was tied to a crossbeam; it appeared to be moving in the air on its own and a group of boys running behind Jonas. But when they caught sight of Cletus they shouted, "Murderer! Murderer!" He was terrified! He had to save his son!

"Cletus, wake up. Wake up!" Claudia was shaken but Cletus was so grateful it was only a dream. His focus on himself and the dream. Now he realized that she was frightened. Had he shouted out while dreaming and frightened her? He started to say it was only a dream. Claudia's voice was trembling. "Look, Cletus!" She pointed to the foot of the bed

Cletus saw blood! Much blood coming from his feet. What was happening now? He threw the bed covers to the floor. More blood! "Claudia, grab the cover and wipe my feet!" Each foot showed a wound that refused to stop bleeding! Claudia sobbed. "Go to the physician!" she pleaded. "Please, Cletus. What is it? What happened? Get dressed and see the physician. Hurry!" She was so frightened! "Did someone come into our room to do this? Who? And why?".

"I don't know, Claudia. But look. See, the bleeding is subsiding. I have no pain. No need for the physician. Find some strips of cotton to bind each foot tightly. That will stop further bleeding," he said with a show of confidence that he really wasn't feeling. As crazy as it seemed Cletus knew without hesitation that this had something to do with yesterday's debacle.

He could not see the physician. How would he explain it? It was true he experienced no pain. He had much to do today before his shift at the prison. He had to quell the bleeding. He couldn't tell those who might notice the blood how it had happened. "Bind them very tightly, Claudia. Here let me do it; I need them tight enough to stop the flow of blood. If anyone asks about the bandages I will say my feet are swollen and I'm trying to keep the swelling down. Probably caused by my new calcis (marching boots)."

You can't go out today like this!" she pleaded.

"I have to, Claudia. I have to find some peace that I can live with. I'll be fine. You'll have to meet Jonas at the Forum. I don't know how my time will be spent today."

What was this thing with the bleeding? How had it happened? Cletus did not understand many things. What did they all mean?

Time to search out Eli. Cletus knew Eli needed to gather information, especially gossip. He suspected Eli would be at the baths today selling his "wares". But Cletus couldn't go to the baths today, not with the bleeding. He didn't really want to waste time at the baths anyway. That meant he had to find the "beggar" before mid-day, eleven o'clock. Maybe Eli would know something about the bleeding and who might have done it. It was more than strange! He hadn't heard anything during the night and even more mystifying he had not found the knife that had been used. Forget the feet. He had to know about The Christ-Jesus-whatever his name was! With the crucifixion just yesterday Cletus thought if anyone had information, real or created to line his money bag, it would be Eli. Cletus was on a mission. He walked the major street in Jerusalem. No luck. No Eli.

He decided his best chance of meeting Eli was the perimeter road. Fear more than time constraint made him hurry. After yesterday's violent storm he was surprised to see so many people were on the road, going on with their lives. Well, wasn't that what he was doing? Trying at least. But Cletus had to understand a few things before he could go on with his life. He had to know! Were these the poor with nowhere specific to go? Were they ill, hurrying to the physician? Or were they like Cletus, trying to expunge an horrendous memory that threatened to plague them forever? Could there be some just out for a stroll with no care in the world? Not his world for sure. And, of course, hundreds of pilgrims from lands far and near crowded the roads for the feast that Jews, by coming to Jerusalem, celebrated every year.

He searched- no Eli. Cletus turned and headed back to the city streets.

As he hurried along he saw him. Titus! Titus saw Cletus but he made no move to approach him. Rather he backed into the shadows. Cletus puzzled, though, "Oh, no you don't brother! You have some explaining to do!" He picked up his pace. Titus didn't move, but waited for Cletus. "That's more like it," Cletus said out loud.

"'Titus, what happened to you yesterday?" Titus looked around and pulled Cletus into the shadows. Cletus had never seen this "cloak and dagger" Titus before. Was he in trouble for yesterday's absence? Was it safe for him to be here? Cletus sensed imminent danger.

What did Titus have to say for himself? "Come to my house. We have to talk. I have something to tell you."

"When? Now?" Cletus asked. Titus merely nodded and walked away. Cletus didn't know why but he waited a few minutes before he stepped out of the shadows and was on his way.

As soon as Titus let him in Cletus pounced. "Titus, you are scaring the hell out of me! What's going on? Are you in some kind of trouble?"

"Well, yes and no."

"Come on, Titus. No theatrics!"

"Cletus, I'm leaving Jerusalem. Tomorrow."

"Are you crazy? Why?"

Titus leaned toward Cletus ready to tell a long tale.

"It's Jesus!"

"You mean The Christ?"

"Yes, but his name, Cletus, is Jesus. Let me tell you my story and then I will answer any questions you have. A few weeks ago our neighbor asked us if we would like to hear the sermons that a very religious man would give at a hill not far out of the city. Normally I wouldn't entertain the idea but the women seemed more excited. I thought it was just another opportunity for our wives to catch up on all the latest gossip, including this "religious" man and his amazing oratory. Miriam was really taken with the idea and begged me to go. So of course we went. The man, who we now know to be Jesus, sat higher from the crowd. He talked mostly about true happiness and identified what you had to do to be truly happy, like be merciful, to be pure of heart, to work for peace- traits like that. It sounded nice. We should all try, right?"

Miriam was ecstatic! So we had to go again. That time was something! We actually got to talk with Jesus. Miriam said a few things but Jesus kept looking at Benjamin. Ben, even though he is twelve years old, felt shy under the gaze of Jesus. Remember, Cletus, the time Ben fell out of that tree two years ago? He put his hands out to catch the fall and he did something to his middle finger? The other boys didn't know how bad it was and they teased him and told him the physician would probably cut it off. Ben was terrified and pleaded with us not to take him to the physician. We looked at it and it was bent a little toward his palm, swollen, but we thought it would heal on its own. But it didn't. Have you seen the hand and finger, Cletus? Well, as we waited for it to heal it ended up completely bent into the palm. There was nothing that could be done and he hasn't been able to use his right hand since. He has learned to keep it turned so it would not be so noticeable. But he can't use the hand to do things other boys do like holding a ball or throwing it.

Well anyway, Jesus reached for Ben and pulled him closer. Jesus turned Ben's finger over and Ben instinctively pulled back. Jesus put his finger under Ben's chin and raised it up so they could look into each others' eyes. Ben held his look until Jesus said, "Spit on your finger, Ben." Jesus stooped down and gathered some dirt. He looked up at Ben again and told him to put the dirt on the spit, to make a paste and rub it on the whole finger. Ben's eyes grew bigger and bigger as his finger slowly lifted and he had full use of it. It was healed!! It was healed, Cletus! Jesus looked on as Ben approached him and embraced him. You can imagine the joy we felt, and Cletus, from that moment I have loved Jesus. We all do. When we got home we sat quietly in a peace I've never felt before.

We went back to be with Jesus again and again. Then we as a family agreed to something. We had to talk to Jesus. I saw a man who seemed to be serving Jesus and told him we would like to dedicate our lives to serving him too. I asked his advice about approaching Jesus. He smiled and said I would know what to say. After the sermon we gathered round Jesus, waiting our turn to speak to Him. I told Him we wanted to serve Him. And we were so thankful for Ben's hand.

Jesus looked into my eyes- oh those eyes!- and asked, "Do you want to follow me because I healed Ben's finger?"

I nodded, unable to speak. The emotion overwhelming. Jesus nodded as well telling me he understood. "I see into your heart Titus," he said. "Are you willing to give up everything to be with me?" My voice returned and I said loud and clear, "We are!" My heart was beating so fast I thought my chest would explode. "We want to be with you because we love you. You are our Lord. We need your father in our lives."

Cletus was confused. The Christ's father was another character to consider. Titus had accepted a role in this drama. The cast of players was clouded in mystery.

"Tears were trickling down my face. Unhurried, Jesus placed His hand on my shoulder and said, "I love you too Titus. You and yours come follow me. The Father knew you before you knew Him." I didn't understand about the Father but to know Jesus is to trust Him even when your ignorance gets in the way."

The plot thickens! Is there any human on earth that perfect?

"We have to go Cletus. Dangerous? Maybe, but Miriam and I have talked and want that peace we felt with Jesus. We need peace in our lives. We don't have it here. We are willing to take the risk. You know what I mean; you and I have talked about it. Always having to be watchful! No matter what happens, with Jesus, there is complete peace.

We know that staying close to Him we have nothing to fear."

Cletus was envious of the peace that was so obvious in Titus-in his home. He silently begged, "I want that peace. I want it! I want it! Maybe this Jesus is the answer."

"And Cletus, what we have been doing in the name of Rome is wrong!"

Cletus was stunned. He believed Titus. He wasn't a religious fanatic. He wasn't weak; he was strong and intimidating in his own way. This Jesus didn't sound like he was a do-gooder, at least if He was, He covered it well, "Titus, was there money involved? Were the people · asked to help support the cause, so to speak?"

Titus sounded a bit miffed but kept his answer neutral and consistent.

"No."

Cletus backed off. This was his best friend. "Titus, what happened yesterday? Where were you during the crucifixion?"

For the first time in their friendship Titus was flustered. "Oh Cletus! My squad was on duty so I was with Jesus all night. I saw Him flogged! I saw Him ridiculed! I saw Him crowned with those damned thorns and I watched as He struggled with His cross! I stayed with Him through it all, trying in some way to ease His pain without drawing too much attention. Why did He not speak up for Himself? I don't know? I struggled from shouting out to defend Him! Then we reached the top of the hill and I saw the crib with the nails for His feet and I just couldn't do it! Pilate be damned; Rome be damned! I wasn't going to do it. I could not torture someone I love! And I will never be a part of killing again. No man deserves what we do to them; even proud that we were hard and ruthless! I'm sorry Cletus but what we have done in the name of Rome, the crucifixions, was wrong and I want no part of it! So yesterday I ran away. I had to! I ran away!" At this Titus broke down and sobbed uncontrollably.

Cletus did not know what to do so he just waited until Titus recovered, at which time he pointed out to Titus how dangerous his plans were. "I know, Cletus, and that is why the girls, Ben, Miriam and I are leaving in darkness. Tomorrow I will not report for assignment. We have to be far from here when they discover I'm gone." Titus stood up as if to signal Cletus to go. Probably a good idea. He could be in trouble too if it were known that he was aware of Titus' plans and had not reported it.

Cletus decided not to tell Titus about the bleeding, Titus had enough to think about. Would he ever see Titus again? Probably not; Cletus had no intention of leaving Jerusalem. Certainly not to chase after a ghost. Titus was his good friend but he was not thinking rationally about this mysterious man.

They embraced and held on longer than was usual. "I love you Cletus." But Cletus couldn't say it. He didn't know how he felt about this love for another man. It didn't feel right. "Yes, me too." Titus had touched him with his enthusiasm; he had to admit. But to run off like criminals? Especially now that Jesus was dead!

How he too longed for peace! He had to be honest. Something or someone was infiltrating his mind, his conscience and his heart. He needed to know more about this Jesus. What was this fickleness? First he wanted to defend his role as a soldier and the next he was drawn to the beauty and peace offered by this unusual man. Cletus knew he couldn't live both. He had to choose. Jesus was able to invade men's minds to make them want to embrace peace and to love one another, bound to attract people who lived in poverty and fear. He suspected that what the poor didn't realize was that some people of power and wealth might seek peace as well. Money cannot buy peace.

He thought about his reactions yesterday, the state of unconsciousness he'd experienced not even hearing The Christ's screams when his hands were nailed and the terror that enveloped him at the agony moment, a stabbing so painful Cletus had nearly collapsed. Who was this man and from where did he get his power? What Cletus didn't know yet; this Jesus would change his life radically.

****

ELI Late Saturday morning

"Well Cletus, my good man, how are you today?"

Cletus knew that weasel voice, "Just great and how are you, Eli?"

"Fine. Fine. Business is a little slow. After the storm yesterday I guess gathering information doesn't seem so urgent." He smiled; it was when he smiled that he looked more like a rat. All that was missing were the whiskers.

"Well Eli, today I am going to contradict you. I'm willing to do business; that is if you have anything to sell. I want information about the twelve men who traveled with The Christ. Where are they? What are their plans?"

The weasel snickered, "Pilate looking for them?"

"Now Ra-um-Eli. You know you're not supposed to know I am gathering information for Pilate. Be cautious, man!"

"Oh right, right. Sorry! But maybe someone besides me knows," he added coyly, hoping to rattle Cletus.

"Now Eli, you know that if I found out you were selling or gifting information regarding our-ahem-partnership I'd have to turn you in to Pilate. He wants this all on the Q T. Don't forget that, Eli!"

Pilate knew nothing of Cletus' involvement with Eli.

"Friends don't put friends in jeopardy," almost mocking Cletus.

Cletus knew him much better than Eli realized. But Cletus had to humor him. Eli's retaliation would be to make up information and sell it for inflated prices, and Cletus could find himself in a mess.

"I know, Eli. Just make sure YOU know."

"Well the death of Jesus is only a day old-little time to know much. Meet me at the market tomorrow and hopefully I'll have something." Tomorrow I work until 10 am. I'll be there shortly after that." Cletus hurried for cleaner air. The weasel headed for the market to play beggar.

****

PRISON LEVEL 1 Sunday Early A.M.

In this heat Cletus found it difficult to appreciate what was usually a small blessing when at guard duty in the prison. Luckily he was assigned to the first level of the underground prison, the only level that had a tiny grated opening, looking out at a major city street. Why it was there nobody knew; but it was there. The small opening promised to change Cletus' life forever!

The busy street offered some diversion for daytime guards and perhaps a prisoner; though unlikely for the incarcerated shackled at the legs, one or both wrists, or neck or even chained to a cell mate. The weight of each chain being about seven pounds. Perhaps there was some relief (or torture) hearing the street sounds of freedom. Night guard duties appealed to soldiers because they did not have to supervise mealtime which was in its own way a kind of torture for the inmates. The only healthy prisoners were those whose family or friends supplemented prison food with more nourishing foods. The poor depending only on prison food often suffered illnesses. Many died in prison due to malnutrition. The amount of food issued to prisoners was half that provided for Roman slaves. The weapon of punishment was the with-holding of food. No baths or haircuts resulted in head lice and incredible stench. There was no advantage for guards on either shift regarding the stench, the nausea attacks harassing guards more than the inmates, especially those inmates who had been there for a while.

Oh, that tiny opening on the first level! It was about 4 inches by 12 inches and right at street level. The opening was grated so nothing could pass in or out of the prison other than air of course. You might think that the sewage troughs, or gutters that were usually along either side of the street would be intolerable, leaving any advantage remote. However the street lining the prison Level 1 was also the street that passed in front of Pilate's residence in Jerusalem. Roman citizens could not abide sewage permeating the air around Pilate and his entourage, so Pilate informed them. Monies were provided and the sewage diverted. So that tiny opening was a chance for the guard to breathe some cleaner air especially at night. The heat being what it was in the city for so long, there was little hope that Cletus would get much relief. He was about 2-3 hours into the shift, around 1 A.M. when he strolled to the opening and peered out.

The moonlight as it played on the opening allowed Cletus to see clearly. He sighed; he was right- no air. What happened next startled him! He saw someone walk past the opening. Of course all he could see were people's feet since the opening was barely street level. It happened so fast! But there was no denying what he saw! Two feet just below a white robe passing by. The feet were bleeding so that the hem of the robe as well as the sandals were stained with blood! The Christ! The Christ!

Cletus ran to the entrance of the prison. A guard was positioned at the entrance to Pilate's home. Cletus knew him. He was Phillip. "Phillip, did you see someone in a white robe walk up the street- that way? Just now?"

"No one has passed since we went on duty at eleven." A reasonable observation. People avoided Pilate's home away from home. They did not want to borrow trouble or to witness someone else's trouble. Likewise Pilate wanted no trouble. Hence the guards. When Pilate was not in Jerusalem no guards were stationed around the court or the adjacent prison, except for some official event being held there.

Cletus did not wait for what Phillip said next. He raced up the street.

Phillip called, "Cletus! Cletus! You can't leave your post! Are you crazy?" Phillip looked in all directions to see if anyone else might have seen what had just transpired. No one.

Cletus couldn't run any further! He was gasping for air, breathing hard. He bent down and put his hands on his knees, lowered his head trying to catch his breath. He'd lost him. He hadn't taken the time to think this through, knowing it was impossible. It just couldn't be! The Christ was dead! He, himself had killed him! He couldn't believe the sorrow he felt, knowing it couldn't be. He finally had his lesson in sorrow. He had been wrong; his imagination punishing him; again another dart piercing his heart! He didn't think there was any heart left for more of this new pain he was enduring. There were many things he questioned; things he did not understand. And for some reason he wanted-NO - he NEEDED to know, and soon!

He hurried back to the prison. If he'd been seen he could find himself chained side by side with those he'd sworn to guard.

Phillip spoke in a loud whisper, "Are you crazy?! Leaving your post!

You can only hope you were not seen!"

"Are you going to report me?"

"Hell no! Get back to your post!"

He was taking too many chances; he realized that. But something was driving him. He wished he could see The Christ again. But how could he? He'd killed The Christ! Murderer!!

****

ELI THE BEGGAR Sunday 10 A. M.

Somehow Cletus had gotten through the night. He was exhausted. But he would not give up. There was something very mysterious about what he'd seen. There was no reasonable explanation for it. Cletus knew The Christ was dead. When you were dead you were dead!

There's no coming back. How he missed Titus; the friend and, yes, the Titus whose peace Cletus longed for. But then Titus had not been a part of death squad. Easy for him to feel peaceful. The murderer felt guilty! Anger was the best defense. And lately Cletus could call upon it easily and quickly! It was near the surface!

Cletus checked the bandages on his feet. No blood. He had observed that his feet did not bleed much during the day; but at night the blood flowed steadily. The bleeding did not affect him in any other way. No dizziness, no fatigue, no nausea- nothing. Claudia worried. What had caused her husband's injury? Actually she worried more about the why and who of it than the injury itself. Cletus was healthy and strong, sure to heal soon. But he was acting very strangely ever since his talk with Jonas. He was a good father, Jonas adored him. It must have bothered him to have comforted his son with what he had insisted were lies.

Washing her hands; drying them on her apron, she was reminded of her own doubts about the honor of some of her husband's duties. Cletus was very impressive in his uniform and demeanor. His family admired him. Pleasing his family was enough to cast aside any misgivings about what he had to do as a soldier. Claudia trusted her husband. Wives were submissive to their husbands and Claudia was comfortable and secure with that.

Cletus' mind was spiraling out of control. He had to recover from this madness. He had to see Eli at the market. He almost ran to get there as soon as possible. He hoped Eli would have some legitimate information that would assist him in his search. For what, he wasn't really sure. He had to think more positively. Eli would have something useful for him. But would Eli also sell the whole scheme to someone who would make Pilate aware? Aloud he said with all the confidence he could muster, "Stop taking your thoughts in this direction, Cletus." He looked around to make sure no one had over-heard him. "Get on with your career as a soldier. Good soldiers follow orders to the letter. They are not murderers. I am not a murderer! I protect Rome by punishing the perpetrators who pursue and threaten the citizens of Rome. A soldier's work is honorable."

Cletus felt somewhat better; he could almost believe his own lies. He approached the market where he hoped Eli would keep their appointment.

Feeling better did not sustain itself. His mind had a different agenda. "Is it honorable to flog 40 lashes minus one for a minor misdemeanor? Is it honorable to torture and insult for sport? Is it honorable to withhold food from prisoners already suffering? Is it honorable to devise, approve and inflict props and procedures whose sole purpose is to prolong suffering and/or death?"

No, Cletus! And o-o-h! Jonas! His greatest guilt was, bar none, he'd convinced Jonas to admire the very things that were wrong! He could ask forgiveness for ignoring the suffering of the prisoners he'd guarded. He might be forgiven for intimidation, for cruelty, for indifference to everything that a decent man would abhor. Honorable men did not nail; an honorable man did not inflict pain; honorable men were not murderers. Perhaps even these could be forgiven. However he was sure teaching a boy to embrace such behaviors as honorable, was too despicable to be forgiven. Cletus would not let Jonas grow to be like his dishonorable father. No more lies! Looking up Cletus was nearing the farmers' market.

"Alms, Sir! Alms for the poor! I'm hungry-alms to buy a meal!" Cletus heard a coin rattle around at the bottom of Eli's tin cup. "Bless you, Sir!"

Cletus turned to see a little bent woman, aged, giving Eli a chunk of her bread. "Bless you, Mother!" She ambled away as Eli tossed the bread into the dirt under the boarded produce stalls behind him.

"Beggar, move on unless you are buying." Cletus shouted his soldierly orders so all could hear. Eli scampered away feigning fear. Cletus sauntered along, not a care in the world. The market hucksters, uneasy, tried to look busy while casting sly glances at Cletus. He chuckled as many soldiers would do to ridicule their fear. Yes, he was good at this "soldier" role! But he could honestly say that neither Titus nor he took pleasure in humiliating those beneath their stature or with prisoners they spent time with as prison guards.

Cletus passed several stalls enjoying the aroma of fresh fruit and freshly baked bread. The distinct fragrance today was olive loaf, his favorite. He spied Eli wedged between two stalls where they would be unnoticed. "You are a despicable man, Eli!" disgust coloring Cletus' words. Eli continued to stare at the horizon to show his indifference.

"Do you have anything for me?" The rat-like grin appeared. "I have information that hikes the price!" Cletus wanted to punch this weasel so badly; but he had to be careful. He couldn't afford to do anything that would dry up the source of possible information. He had to maintain this partnership, at least until he had learned as much as he could about The Christ's followers.

Eli took his time answering. No one was as interesting as Cletus angry or frustrated. "Jesus' followers are hanging around the vine-covered wool smith's shop outside the city. Don't know where they stay at night. They appear in long cloaks with hoods which they wear day and night. They fear being captured by one of you stalking them for Pilate. Hey, is this what you are doing, trying to bring them to Pilate?" During their whispered exchange Eli would periodically and stealthily check for any possible audience. No one nearby.

"You needn't worry, Eli; I'm not bringing YOU in. That's all you need to know." Cletus hoped the threat would insure Eli's silence.

It was obvious that Eli wanted to get back to "work". He wasn't any happier to be seen with Cletus. He did not want any of his other customers to see them. He tried to keep his regulars from knowing each other. They tended to clam up. Suspicious about how their involvement might be passed along, especially to a soldier. "There was some talk about a meeting the followers are trying to set up."

Cletus jumped at that. Eli thought he would and snickered, exposing his teeth; narrow and sharp. Cletus narrowed the distance between them. "Where? When?"

"Don't know. It's just rumor right now." And he backed away.

"Eli, I'll meet up with you every day to see if you hear any more. In the mean time you get me a cloak exactly like theirs. There will be something extra, maybe very impressive, if you take care of the added request s and keep all of this to yourself. Any customers I over-ride I'll make it worth your while."

That got Eli's attention! He grinned, almost drooling. "Of course, Cletus. I know you do your work for Pilate and you are an honest man. You can count on me. I must go before venders wonder where I am. I usually stay until mid-day Forum. I'll find the cloak you want."

He left Cletus to choreograph next moves for whatever Pilate had assigned him. Rubbing his hands together he whispered, "Talk about "cloak and dagger!" He giggled at his joke, "Cloak, hee, hee!"

"Eli, how much?" Cletus shouted out to the beggar.

He skittered back. "The usual." Cletus dropped a coin in Eli's extended hand. In a blink of an eye Eli balled his hand into a fist as if Cletus might change his mind and snatch it back.

Despite his brooding, Cletus chuckled, shaking his head. "Oh, Beggar you are so predictable!"

****

PILATE Sunday A.M.

Cletus had spent most of the day loitering around the wool smith's shop. He did not dress in the cloak today but he kept it near in case he needed it; he couldn't imagine any scenario in which he would don the hooded cloak worn by the followers. But he masqueraded among the poor dressed with garments and other gear he had pilfered from the prison. His tunic, a long shirt, was the regular wear of the poor. All the peasants living here were poor. Their homes were shabby enclosures; but even here were some who, though poor, took pride in their possessions. They were stubbornly clean. Both clothing and homes. Some even had trellises for grapes surrounded with simple crops to sell as well as for their own diets. These were few and far between. Several times of the day women were sweeping the floors of the sand that was no respecter of class or cleanliness.

Cletus tried to avoid interactions with the men, who expected an explanation of the new resident to their neighborhood. His story was that he lived in the nearby hills but was waiting for a traveling relative, told to meet him near the wool smith's shop. And of course traveling such as it was around Jerusalem, especially at festival time, it was difficult to pin down arrival. Thus Cletus, would be there until such time as his relative arrived. Could be days. Cletus had to be very alert; he did not want to be spotted by a soldier, who'd accompany him to Pilate's interrogation room. Soldiers were not expected to be seen in this area unless on assignment, but it was possible. Cletus knew he had to be careful.

There was no history of an accused traitor who had proven his innocence, not one on record. Traitors, either in or out of the military were guilty, with no opportunity to prove innocence. All in the military were aware that bonuses were awarded for reporting any soldier of wrong-doing; a tempting incentive for creating falsehoods for gain. So Cletus definitely did not want to meet up with another soldier.

Having had no breakfast he was hungry. But there was no way he'd look for food in this area; the menu among the poor was mainly mice and peacock tongue. He was tempted to give up and go to the market and get something to eat. He'd seen nothing of import. No one on the roads was dressed in hooded cloaks. He decided to leave for a breakfast at the market.

Maybe he'd hear something from Eli. He left his disguise in a barrel behind the wool smith's shop and set out to find something to eat.

With his appetite satisfied on 2 large chunks of olive bread dripping with honey and no sight of Eli he decided to head on home. He still couldn't go to the baths. No bleeding to speak of, but the sores were quite visible, impossible to come up with a believable explanation. He was on duty tonight. His state of mind left him exhausted; he needed to rest. He hurried through the city. He did not want to meet anyone.

With the unfamiliar stretch of road ahead of him Cletus realized that for the first time in his life, in Jerusalem, he will have traveled the entire perimeter of dirt road surrounding the city. Men of the elite never went about using this road; soldiers only when an assignment required expediency via the perimeter road. Cletus encountered only a few others along the way. For some reason as he strolled quietly, he felt a little calmer. Not free but calmer. In the quietness his mind was less cluttered-perhaps a good omen.

Ahead, in the bright sunshine stood a copse of trees cradling the road meandering under and through it. As though intentional the copse formed a row of trees on both sides of the road. Branches reaching across to each other as lovers might reach out to hold hands, forming a canopy effect over the dirt path; clasping hands, swinging and swaying, creating a cooling effect for the travelers below, under their cloud of green. Cletus slowed his pace to prolong this blessed serenity. He knew it would be short-lived. Still slower capturing all he could of it. Studying it as he would a painting on canvas he noticed an odd phenomenon. Strangely as people stepped under the canopy they slowed their pace as though they found a contentment that wasn't felt on the open road, the sun beating down on them. Giving way to the imagination it became a spiritual enclosure. It was impossible to resist; they looked up, out-stretched their arms, like men praying in the temple. Exiting the other end more peaceful and content. Cletus embraced the illusionary metaphor.

"Oh, if it were only that easy," Cletus thought. If it were true he would erect a tent and live his life there under the trees. He would exchange ideas and thoughts with travelers, offering a vessel of cool water to quench their thirst. They would nod in respect for each other. They'd move on refreshed.

"Refreshed!" Yes! That's what Cletus wanted so badly, refreshed in peace. "Please!. Please! The serenity cannot be a mirage!" And Cletus for the first time believed peace was possible; sometimes found in mysterious ways and places. He definitely would return to this magical place. "Open your heart when you open your eyes, Cletus!" he told himself. He was certain the man they called Jesus was a magician creating peace in awesome places. And for those he chose. Jesus somehow was at the center of peace.

He had to attend that meeting of the followers. He had to learn from them how it was done. He missed Titus. He'd know what to do; his friendship would support and help Cletus. Peace will come-it has to. These thoughts plagued him day and night.

"Just breathe slowly and deeply and walk on home." Cletus ordered himself.

"Cletus! Cletus!" He turned around to see another soldier, one he knew only by sight.

"I've been ordered to bring you to Pilate."

Cletus' heart took a dive. Someone had turned him in! "Why does Pilate want to see me?"

"I don't know, Man. I'm just the messenger. Please come with me."

So much for a good omen!

His heart was racing so fast he thought he might die on the way! Silently his mind was on Jonas and Claudia, "Oh, Jonas, I'm sorry, Son! All those things about a good soldier. Don't believe them, Son! I lied to you! I'm sorry; I wanted to be your hero. And Claudia, I'm torn apart thinking of the shame I've brought to you. Unfortunately you were paired with me, the best thing that happened to me. And the worst thing that has happened to you. I'm so sorry!" Cletus refused to hang his head before citizens on the road. He was still a soldier, however briefly, and he'd hold his head high until he was no longer one.

They entered a small room, lavishly appointed. Large palm leaves were clustered together moving to cool the air. A slave in an adjacent room operated the movement by lowering and raising the leaves hanging from a satin braided rope. This was not the interrogation room. That confused Cletus but he knew better than to speak until spoken to.

Pilate held up the peasant clothes Cletus had discarded earlier. Cletus' face flushed a bright red. He hoped this sign of guilt would not give him away.

"Because I've held you in high esteem, Cletus, I will hear you out." It was evident that the compliment Pilate had given was two-fold. Also a warning of Pilate's position and power. In the event he had to revise his position on the subject, that is if Cletus could not explain himself to Pilate's satisfaction.

Cletus had to save himself. "Think quickly!" he told himself.

"As you know I was on the squad for the crucifixion of The Christ. I lingered after the crowd had dispersed. I saw his mother grieving at the foot of the upright. There was a man with her that I felt uncomfortable about, as if he were planning something. He was strong and seemed eager to pursue other concerns. He was hurrying the women along. It was clear to me that he was angry.

It was just a hunch but I was suspicious. I had heard that twelve were planning a meeting. To satisfy my curiosity I decided to go to the outskirts of the city dressed as one of them, to see if I could spot them or, at least, hear any gossip concerning them. But no luck seeing them. From all the gossip I have heard the followers have left the city. Since I was wrong about the man, I saw no need to report."

"Hm, interesting," Pilate paced the room. "Well at least you found them gone. It is difficult to imagine that a handful of peasants could be a threat to Rome.

However you made one mistake, Cletus. NEVER assume there is no need to report. I order you to remember that. The next time you get – what did you call it? A hunch! REPORT it!"

Cletus bowed hoping to be dismissed. A nod told him Pilate was finished with him. He walked toward home. He was drained! He'd been dismissed with just a slap on the wrist, unheard of! He was going to keep this incident to himself. He knew he was treading in deep waters. But that did not deter him. He was still going to find out what the meeting was about.

Pilate turned to soldiers stationed at his door. "Follow him. He knows something he isn't telling me. Stay on him until I call you in. Keep your eyes on him at all times. I want information about the so-called meeting." Pilate turned his back, indicating that they were dismissed. They bowed as one and backed out facing Pilate, and bowing intermittently.

Like good soldiers they would not let Cletus out of their sight. One of them, a not so good soldier, schemed, "No need to stay on him. When the time is right we can provide information and evidence to Pilate and receive our bonus."

"Sounds good to me. Friend, we have some time off as long as we are occasionally seen around the wool smith's shop." They headed for the baths. Maybe they'd see Cletus there.

No Cletus. Oh well. A good long massage was called for. They were s-o-o over-worked! They were grinning as they plunged into the cold pool.

While Cletus and the other soldiers were scheming their next moves, Pilate mulled over these events. "I'll use Cletus to take the chances and do the dirty work, gathering what I want to know. Then will be soon enough to strip him of his military standing." As a lesson to others he'd make an example of Cletus. His shame and dishonorable discharge would take place at the up-coming military assembly! "I should have told him to keep his disguise; he'll need it for his future wardrobe!" He retired to his lounge.

Pilate was pompous and cruel. He reached for his goblet of wine, lounged back lazily, sighed and sipped. Smiling arrogantly he raised his goblet and toasted, "Jerusalem, long live your sovereign governor!"

****

THE CHRIST Days later

Eli comes through! He had gathered more news than Cletus needed; gossip of little consequence. Cletus is also sly when it's called for and he doesn't want Eli to ascertain what to share and with whom. So he was willing to pay for non-productive information so Eli's greed would entice him to dig deeper and snoop harder- any little tidbits. Cletus was wise to Eli's trickery, knowing he held loyalty as insignificant. Loyalty was not something he could sell, definitely not a commodity. Eli felt no remorse that his information, either true or falsehoods, might result in consequences costly for other human beings- dishonor, sorrow, injury or even murder or death. He simply didn't care; he was a totally despicable man. Cletus hated doing business with him but he was driven. By what- he didn't know. But by WHOM- he was sure!

As darkness settled over Jerusalem the followers were beginning to arrive for the meeting, trickling two or three at a time. Cletus was dressed in peasant clothes, again from the prison. He was hardly noticed by the hooded men. They seemed fearful, worried and anxious. None had entered the house where they lingered. Eli had told Cletus that the follower named Judas had been found hanging from a tree, dead![5] So only eleven were among the followers.

Then Cletus heard something that set his imagination on fire! One of the cloaked men whispered, unaware he had been heard, "Thomas will not be here tonight." Cletus saw his opportunity to find out more about The Christ. None of the men chanced being identified; their hoods hiding their faces. Cletus could fill-in for Thomas. This was the most confident he'd felt since the beginning of all this crucifixion. But he had to be very careful. What if, once they were all inside, they removed their hoods? If caught he might be killed for all he knew. But if these men had Titus' peace, he thought he would be safe. He begged to remain with these men long enough to find how to earn his. The Christ was the key. These men knew The Christ personally. He could learn much from them, hopefully tonight. He quickly left his post in the front of the house.

Back again Cletus simply joined the group crowding around the door. No one spoke to him and he breathed easier. He pulled his hood down and close to his face. His heart pounded! He was trembling! Might he really get away with this? He had to! For Jonas. For Claudia. And, yes, for himself.

Cletus waited to be last to enter the house. The door opened and the men hurried in.

What Cletus saw changed him forever! It can't be! Impossible! It just cannot be! His heart tightened in his chest.

He saw The Christ greeting each apostle by placing His hand on their shoulder. He said not a word; He smiled to let each know he was a precious friend. To ease their anxiety.

Cletus found it difficult to breathe. He never thought of running away. He couldn't. Slowly, step by step, man by man he inched closer and closer to The Christ. He couldn't have looked away from The Christ if his life depended upon it. Cletus would soon find that indeed his life DID depend upon it!

The man in front of Cletus moved away. Cletus did not shrink. He'd do whatever he needed. The Christ would have to address him.

The Christ nodded and smiled. Those boys in the playground were right. The Christ smiled a lot! "Don't touch me, Cletus. You cannot stay." Again Cletus' heart told him what sorrow really is. He could not turn away. He knew when he did the peace would drift away. How he longed to stay with this man!

The Christ nodded; he understood. "You cannot be here. But I will come for you soon.

"When? Where?!"

"I will come. My Father wants me to talk to you. Go now and believe! Continue to work as a soldier until we talk again. It will be alright."

Cletus looked doubtful. Jesus knew. "Pilate will not summon you. My Father has taken care of everything. Don't be afraid."

The Christ turned away from him. As Cletus left all he could do was to close the door quietly, knowing it protected something precious, keeping The Christ safe.

Cletus DID believe. No one lived beyond death, yet he believed.

He took his time going home. He needed to think; how to tell Claudia of this amazing night. He felt as if he were floating on a cloud. To his amazement his heart was whole again. He laughed because he was no longer heartless!

"The Father wants The Christ to talk to me!" He hadn't considered being nervous. Because The Christ was The Father's son. They came as one!

To The Christ, to his Father, Cletus whispered, "Thank you," as tears fell softly on his cheeks.

****

AT HOME Same night

Cletus was exhausted! As Claudia brushed her hair, a nightly routine, Cletus readied for bed. He unwound the bandages from his feet. At what he saw this time, he shouted to his wife, "Claudia, look!" Not only had the bleeding stopped but there were no sores or scars! No evidence of an injury!

Claudia and Cletus lay together in a peace that promised to consume them. Cletus silently heaped praise on The Christ. Again, he was a non-prayer who was praying.

****

JESUS Several weeks later

Maybe he wasn't coming. No one on the grapevine even discussed The Christ any more. They all thought him dead. No longer a source of gossip. Cletus was anxious. What if he were assigned a crucifixion? He couldn't; he wouldn't participate! He would be in prison immediately! A soldier follows orders without question.

Cletus pleaded, "Please, The Christ; please The Father. Come soon. Come today!" Cletus was praying again. He'd never prayed before The Christ came into his life. He didn't know how. As in all men Cletus instinctively prayed without knowing it. Those who didn't know Or accept the one true God might call it hope. Hoping only in yourself without God was useless and could not be trusted. It often led to bitter disappointment and life changes they'd later regret. Simply because they chose not to believe or were ignorant of the possibilities in knowing and accepting God.

Cletus knew that only with Christ could hope and peace continue in his life. His resurrection the only true HOPE! Peace came only in knowing and serving Him.

Cletus found himself more and more anxious with each day of waiting. "He told me to be patient. I'm trying to be."

Often he'd glimpsed Claudia sitting quietly, head bowed, hands folded in her lap. Tendrils escaping from the pile of hair she had twisted in a roll atop her head formed ringlets of curls. Cletus preferred it long to her shoulders but appreciated it was not practical as she went about her daily work. She was lovely either way. A delicate smile on her face reminded him of The Christ's mother as he had approached her under the cross. She knew he was the one who'd pounded the nails into her son's feet; yet she showed no hatred or anger toward her son's executioner. She simply smiled and lowered her head again.

Today Claudia looked up and saw him gazing at her. "What?" she asked as she came to him and placed her hands on his chest. "You brought this peace to our home and lives. What better can a man do for his family?" She stood on tiptoes and kissed his cheek, turned, and went back to her womanly work.

Cletus expelled a trembling sigh. He was still a Roman soldier and old training and demeanor often took advantage of a chink in his armor and spilled out, sending darts of anger and ridicule at the prisoners he guarded. His misplaced anger led to haughtiness in dealing with any common citizens. He wanted them to continue to fear and avoid him.

At night as he lay in bed, he asked forgiveness for his short resolve; perhaps the reason Jesus hadn't come. "He must be disappointed in how quickly I've failed. Some dedicated servant I am! He couldn't want me now. There is no place for a Roman soldier in the life Jesus expected. He wouldn't be sure He could depend on me!"

Tears fell as Cletus rolled away from Claudia who slept peacefully beside him. "Just what Jesus needs, a cry baby!"

Doubts continued to plague him during more days of waiting. "Jesus, come soon! Save me from myself!" But then maybe He wasn't coming after all. Cletus began to question his worthiness. And it was lacking. If Jesus knew Cletus' true character, he wouldn't show up. Not the kind of man He and his Father would want.

Claudia thrived on the peace her husband was fighting for. She didn't know much about this Jesus but she trusted her husband. If leaving was what Cletus needed for them, she'd go and trust this holy man and his friends, who only a few weeks ago were the topic of many gossip mongers.

Cletus and Claudia had decided to keep their plans from Jonas until they knew what Jesus wanted of them. They were prepared for leaving Jerusalem and would decide how and what they'd tell him at that time. It saddened and ate away at Cletus that Jonas still thought of The Christ as a threat to Jerusalem. He still admired his father's "protection" by his participation in the crucifixion.

Again Cletus stepped out on the road and shaded his eyes. No Jesus!

From behind he heard, "Come sit with me, Cletus. I must talk to you." Cletus spun around! His heart soared! He is here!!

As Cletus approached The Christ who was sitting under an olive tree, he asked, "May I call you Lord? I know Titus does."

"Yes, if you believe I am."

Cletus responded, "I believe you are my Lord if you want me."

I DO want you. As for who I am, I am my Father's son. My name is Jesus, among other names. Do not call me The Christ. Brothers call brothers by name. All the while Jesus twirled a simple clover as though examining it. Almost to Himself he muttered, "My Father created such beautiful wonders. Even a simple clover speaks of my Father's gift of artistry." Finally He looked up, making sure Cletus was not upset with his rather stern retort regarding His name. Again Jesus smiled. Sheer joy spilled like sunshine over Cletus. His hands refused to stop trembling.

Sit down with me, Cletus." Cletus slipped to the grass, remained silent. They looked into each other's eyes. Jesus smiled! Cletus smiled! Love continued its journey into his heart. They were both silent for a few moments. Cletus was more nervous than he wanted to be, but the arrow of peace continued to hit its target. Silence! Guilt wormed its way back into Cletus' heart despite the love. Cletus did not feel worthy regardless of what his heart felt. He hung his head.

"I know you have worries, Cletus. Please give them to ME."

"Truth! Only the truth!" Cletus said to himself.

He began, "You say you want me. Well, you don't really know me."

Jesus said quietly, "I doubt that. But tell me, Cletus."

Cletus swallowed with effort. Jesus watched his Adam's apple move up and down as Cletus labored for courage to speak. His resolve pushed him forward. He shared how the soldier in him still surfaced and he often struck out, hurting those who were not really responsible. "I berated the prisoners. I used my old strength and demeanor as a soldier. I wanted others to look up to me for my fearlessness. Do you believe I feel that way even after you loved me enough to come for me. I don't deserve your love."

"Too bad," Jesus smiled," since I choose to love everyone. You CANNOT stop me from loving you. Are you truly sorry for these things?"

Again he hung his head and nodded silently. But he had more to tell.

"But," Cletus began again, "my son! The things I've allowed him to believe by my fatherly talks with him as his role model. A role model for lying, for valuing a man's life in such low esteem, for killing, for untrue justification of force and fear!!" He sobbed, "He admires me for all the wrong things! I'm responsible. I'm so frightened he will grow up to be the man he thinks I am!" Cletus nearly shouted out, "I need to prevent that from happening. Please help me, Lord!"

Jesus replied, "I will help you, I promise. My Father's plan will take care of all of it, if you live the life we ask of you. It is our covenant with you."

Cletus stopped trembling. Silently he nodded and whispered, "Thank you! I need you. I want to be as you are; you IN me." Then he fell silent again.

Jesus so loved this man before him; he waited.

"There's something else."

His Lord replied, "I know but give it to ME."

"It is my ego and pride." Sheepishly he said, "I like being looked up to people fearing me-well, not really fearing me- but rather respecting me. That swells me up with pride. I like being awarded for bravery, for my wisdom, I like people to know I was hand-picked for crucifixion and other special assignments. I like having a beautiful woman on my arm, so others will admire me. I like attention. Before you say you want me, you need to know all these things about me. I don't want you to be disappointed in me." He let out a long breath as though he hadn't breathed during this admission.

Jesus said nothing yet. He smiled and thought, "Oh, Cletus you don't really know me either."

"Cletus, my Father knows your heart is heavy with guilt. He wants you to know that you were part of his plan for the world, as long as it exists. You see I was sacrificed for the sins of the world, and to save man from death. And to insure that His will would be accomplished, some had to further His plan. Among others Judas was one of those chosen and you were another. But both of you were free to accept or reject that role You accepted until my Father opened your heart. Do you see, Cletus? Judas did not ask for forgiveness. You DID!

No he did not understand. "But I was the murderer!"

Jesus tried to help him understand. "There were two men on the road who encountered another man traveling alone. They decided to beat the man until he would give up his money bag. They took the money bag and left the man to die. They divided the coins between them and parted.

The first robber thought, "We didn't have to beat him. I feel bad but it's too late to undo it." And he continued down the road clutching the coins, dreaming of his plans to use them.

The second robber was feeling guilty. He had pummeled and kicked the man. He returned and nursed the victim back to good health. He also gave back his half of the money bag. He said, "I'm sorry. Forgive me for hurting you." And they continued on their way. "Now which of these two robbers was worthy of forgiveness?"

"I had to die on the cross so sins could be forgiven. My Father loves you, Cletus. He has sent me into the world to forgive sins. And he sends me to you especially. He knows that you are sorry for your part in my death and you want forgiveness. He also believes you are sorry for your life as a soldier. ARE you sorry for all the sins throughout your life?" Cletus just hung his head in sorrow. He was sorry. Jesus knew that.

My Father chooses those who deserve forgiveness. He never tires of forgiving.[2]

My Father is Love. You must be put right with Him. Stand up, Cletus." They both stood, Jesus placed one hand on Cletus' head and the other on his shoulder.

"All your sins are forgiven you, Cletus. And when God forgives your sins they are forgotten. You have helped bring hope and forgiveness into the world. My Father blesses you and yours and loves your prayers of gratitude. You have many qualities pleasing to God and He loves you. He is with you and He will give you the peace you are looking for and the strength to live as He would have you do.

You are strong. You have passion. You strive to excel. You know you are a role model. Use all these things to accomplish GOOD. My Father will work through you. Don't be afraid; go to Him; He is waiting for you; He will take care of everything.

"You are put right with my Father." Cletus tried to hide his tears of joy.

Jesus fell silent, giving Cletus the glorious luxury of His Father's love and fforgiveness.[2]

"There are no situations which God cannot change;......[3] I have little time left, so first I must ask you. Will you love and serve my Father?" Cletus nodded vigorously.

"Take your family to the home of my mother and a young man named John. Do not take anything with you; my Father will provide all that you need. You will be safe there, Cletus.

I want you to protect my mother and John. For her protection I have asked my Father to assign you to her. Your soldier's training will serve you well, keeping my mother from harm. Direct your failings to good purpose. I want my mother to be free of fear; she's gone through so much. Take care of her, Cletus. She will help Claudia to learn about my Father and me; just as you will have John. I want them and their home secure. Do this in my name."

"I will!"

"John will share all he has learned about me and my Father. John will help you know Him. He who created the world and all that is in it. You will know Him and you will love Him. My Father is the only true God and He loves you. John will also help you pray. You are much closer than you know. While you are staying with John and my mother you must share your story with other followers who come there. Wash their feet. Do not be afraid to admit to being a former soldier; my Father will protect you from the Roman government.

You like attention and you will have it as long as you tell all you meet that your strengths come from God. Give God the credit. Without Him you have no strengths. Thank God every day for all the good you can do because of him.

Jonas .... Jonas will see his father change right before his eyes. He will see love, compassion and, yes strength-strength to do all that is good. He will see John and visitors living the life his father lives. There will be love, Cletus. Jonas is smart; he will absorb it all and admire you. He will begin to do the same things, his father a great role-model. He will come to you and you will teach him to love, to pray, to honor all that is good and to know my Father and me. Will you love and serve my Father, Cletus?"

"YES, yes I do and I will." It was very complicated but he believed. There was so much to learn. Cletus no longer felt alone and was certain that with Jesus and the Father he never would be again.

Jesus smiled and bowed his head and whispered, "Thank you Father."

Cletus didn't hear him, he was so caught up in his own thoughts.

"When it is time you will go to Joppa as an apprentice to a tanner named Simon. It will be back-breaking work. But We will always be with you. You will learn to tan the hides and make sandals. You will open your own shop and will tell your story to anyone who wants to hear it. If they won't listen fit them in your finest sandals and send them on their way. Your shop will be a safe haven for my followers. From this day forward your name will be Sutor (which means shoemaker.)

In the meanwhile greet all weary travelers who come to John's and tell them about the God you serve. Tell them your story. Let your pride be in your humility. Because without God there is no story to tell.

Your mission is to open God's door to all and to be the presence of God's love.

And, Sutor, my Father works in His own time, so be patient."

"Tell Him, Lord, that I said Thank You."

"You tell Him, Sutor." A pause that felt so final! "And, Sutor, I will not see you again until you enter into my Father's kingdom. I have to go now."

"Lord, please don't!"

Jesus stood, smiled and embraced him. "I WILL come again. Watch for me. John will talk to you of my coming."

Sutor's heart was breaking. His time with Jesus was coming to an end; yet it sang with joy and praise for the love of Jesus and God the Father. "MY Lord, I love you."

Jesus remained silent and looked deep into his friend's eyes. could drown in them. The joy he felt shattered his guilt! He was forgiven! His heart sang ..... PEACE PEACE PEACE

And then He was gone.............

****

SUTOR TEN YEARS LATER

Just outside of Joppa weary travelers, a man leading a donkey and a woman sitting upon it, trudged along approaching a shop that boasted a sign:

SUTOR'S SANDALS

In front of the shop stood a man shading his eyes from the first rays of the setting sun. As they drew nearer they noticed the man was holding a sandal with a beautifully tooled design:

The shopkeeper smiled displaying wrinkles that actually made him more handsome. His upper body was muscular, likely the result of grueling hard labor. All in all a fine specimen of a man.

He questioned the travelers, "Where are you heading? You look as though you've been on the road for some time."

The tall man explained they planned to spend the night at an inn, hoping there was one in Joppa. His wife was weary and needed rest from the dusty roads.

The shop keeper, whom they assumed was Sutor, shook his head. "It is very expensive at the Joppa Inn. My home is open to you for lodging and you can join us for evening meal.

The stranger did not respond immediately. He looked to the woman on the donkey. She nodded.

"What do you charge?"

"Oh, there is no charge. But one requirement. After meal you must listen to a story I have to tell you. It is my story.

"Sounds fair. What kind of story?"

Sutor explained, "For me, the greatest story ever told. And after I've told it, you must share it with someone else, if you believe. If not, I'll still put you up for the night and morning meal before you set out again. I'll throw in a pair of sandals. The stranger smiled and nodded his assent.

Sutor laughed and turned to the shop. He pointed to the pasture, "Oh, that is my son leading our cow to the stable for evening milking. My daughter, Hannah, though only five years old, is helping her mother prepare the evening meal. Come. Welcome."

His smile was hard to resist and his travelers smiled in return.

"Come my brother and I will wash your weary feet."

As they entered the shop leading to their host's home, Sutor turned over a sign on the door:

Closed To No One
Please Knock

****

SUTOR'S DAILY PRAYER

Great and loving God, I would like with all my heart to experience your immense love and to be changed-- made new---so that I can see your hand in all things. Thank you for the gift of faith. I know that I am often self-centered, O God, especially when I do good deeds and expect something in return. Even when I pray, I sometimes think of myself as good and holy. But all goodness comes from you. Help me to believe this and to open my heart to you more fully. Sprinkle my heart and cleanse me from anything that keeps me from loving and serving you. I want to pass on my faith by living it. Help me to hold on to what is good and to share that goodness freely with those I meet. Please deepen my faith each day of my life journey. Thank you for your son, Jesus Christ in whose name I have been baptized. Today I will recall that Jesus walks with me always, and when I share this belief with others I am keeping the memory of him alive.[2]

Bless my family and keep them safe. I thank you for Claudia, Hannah, and Jonas. Your blessings sustain us. All honor, glory and praise to you O Lord. I ask this in Jesus' name. Amen.

Walking with Pope Francis
30 Days with the ENCYCLICAL
The Light of Faith

AUTHOR' NOTE

Because I have a special love for Pope Francis I share his thoughts:

When we seek Jesus, we discover that
he is waiting to welcome us,
To offer his love. And this fills your
heart with such wonder that you
Can hardly believe it, and this is how
your faith grows---through
Encounter with a Person, through
encounter with the Lord. It is
important to read about faith, but
look, on its own this is not
enough! What is important is our
encounter with Jesus, our encounter
with him, and this is what gives
you faith, because he is the
One who gives it to you!

POPE FRANCIS SPEAKS TO OUR HEARTS Words
of Challenge and Hope Published by Word Among Us

ANGEL

**A Short Story
By
Mary Jane Casey Lane**

It was an amazingly easy pregnancy. Literally no morning sickness, nausea or depression, sometimes a problem I'm told, but absolutely no tears or moodiness. I gained only 24 pounds and felt like a million bucks! John and I wanted a baby so badly and were over-joyed when we found we were pregnant.

The only chink in the nine exciting months was a very active baby- turning, twisting and kicking. We joked that I should probably begin training for the Boston Marathon in preparation for the Terrible Twos. No hurry 'til two, after all how over-active could a new-born be? Oh, but when we saw her, her tiny fist wrapped around our pinky, there was no further joking. She was beautiful, a chubby bundle (7 pounds even), topped with a mass of curls, smiling and obviously happy in the world we'd begun to build for her. Soon after birth she'd begun to sleep the night through. Strangely when most mothers longed for a full night's sleep, I'd dream of nighttime feeding and a walk around in the dark trying to coo her back to sleep. When I couldn't sleep, roaming from room to room I'd almost wished she would wake up so I could hold her; I craved the cuddling she gave so sweetly and so often. But she slept at night and that's the way it was. She was happy to cuddle with her daddy as well. Who'd believe that a new-born could control the dynamics of the family? But she certainly did! With more to come.

She showed no reluctance for friends and family members. She enjoyed each silly face they gave, encouraging them to be even more foolish. She tolerated the baby talk and rewarded all with a beautiful smile. We named her Angela and soon began to call her Angel because she **was** an angel. Perfect! John and I talked about how unbelievably fortunate we were to have this child of God.

Cleaning the kitchen from yesterday's third birthday party, I appreciated yet again the window over the sink. When we'd bought our home the window seemed to add to the charm of the colonial house. I loved looking out as I did the dishes, admiring the two oak trees near the back fence in full maturity and my favorite tree, the weeping willow. As a child I had played under the weepings, pretending it was Sherwood Forest and I was Maid Marian. My brother was the daring Robin Hood. Angel never played near the willow because it was the gathering place for mosquitoes, as though it were their duty to guard it against invaders. I could watch over my three-year-old as she played in our comfortable back yard beyond my window. She always seemed to be happy to be alone in play, drawing from her vivid imagination. We were not concerned that she was usually happier playing alone because she played with other children from our family and friends as well when the opportunity presented its self.

Today she sat at her small-fry table and chairs pouring water-tea in the tiny cup in front of her teddy bear guest. She talked through the scene creating her own script. I loved watching her but I had an idea. I grabbed a plastic birthday plate and covered it with Ritz crackers. I took it out to the yard.

"Angel, here is your dessert for Teddy."

"What is it, Mommy?"

"Napoleons."

"What are poleons? They look like crackers."

I laugh. She studies my face for a second. Then she laughs too and skips back to her tea party. I hear, "Poleons for dessert, Teddy, but they look like crackers."

My heart swells. Then the kitchen called to me again and I dug in. An hour later I was surprised how long I'd been working. I checked the yard again. Angel was under the little table searching for what- I don't know. If I asked she'd probably say she saw a diamond and was trying to find it. I smiled but it was past time for her nap. I opened the window and called to her. "Angel, time for your nap." She came without hesitation; she always obeyed without complaint. Sometimes when I thought how perfect she was, I was almost frightened. Silly. I reminded myself to thank God for our life with this perfect little creature.

As she turned into the kitchen the glass I was drying slipped through my fingers, hit the tile, smashing into a myriad of glass shards. Afraid Angel might try to walk over it, I shouted, "Stay back Angel! You'll be cut!" I looked at her and she was staring at me. I had never seen that look before. For some reason I felt compelled to keep staring back. Finally she said, "Oh, Mommy, you're BAD. You broke the glass. You are BAD!" For a moment I knew the taste of guilt. Ridiculous! Just as quickly I saw how stupid that was; she is just a baby. I'd scared her with my urgency to keep her away from the broken glass. And she doesn't know the difference between an accident and something intentional.

"Sweetheart, it was just an accident. I didn't mean to break the glass. Come on, let's get you in for your nap. You played a long time today. I'll clean up the floor while you nap. Okay?"

"Yes Mommy -but you were BAD." I did not respond. This conversation was over. There will be no more "bad" talk. It isn't good for her to think that way. John and I had decided to steer any correction language in positive wording. We never used the words "sin", "bad" or "naughty".

I cleaned up the glass and began preparations for dinner. John would be home in an hour or so. I was making a chicken casserole (one of John's favorite meals). A green salad and chocolate pudding (Angel's favorite dessert).

What red-blooded American child did not like chocolate? Whereas Angel was so easy to live with she was very particular about her food. She would not even try a bite of green beans or fish or anything she decided would not taste good to her. Of what she did like she ate healthy portions so we didn't push. And the doctor told us not to worry and even suggested we serve foods we liked even though she didn't. He assured us that if she were hungry she'd eat something. And we shouldn't worry if occasionally she missed a meal.

"Mommy, I awake. Mommy. Mommy."

"I'm coming, Sweetie." I loved seeing her arms outstretched toward me. I lifted her out of her crib, nuzzled her neck and kissed her cheek. I swept away a curl dangling over her eyes. "Did my little angel have a good nap?" She nodded and dug her little fist into her eyes to chase away the sleep. "Let's get you washed up and in a clean pinafore before Daddy gets home, shall we?" She nodded.

"Daddy will probly bring me something," she said hopefully.

"He may not, sweetie. You can't have something every night. Just on special nights. Like yesterday for your birthday."

"I think he probly will." She said confidently. Oh, well if she was disappointed, maybe that would be a good lesson for her to experience.

While I worked on dinner Angel put together a wooden puzzle she had received as a birthday gift.

"Hello, are my girls here?" John entered from the garage entrance.

"Daddy!" Angel screamed as she threw herself into his arms. "Did you bring me something, Daddy?"

"Now, Angel, you can't get something everyday."

"That's okay, Daddy!" That's our sweet little girl. I smiled. John looked over at me and smiled too. She brings us such joy and makes us so proud.

Angel took both hands and turned her father's face so he'd look right into hers. "Daddy, Mommy was bad today!" John, puzzled, looked at me and raised his eyebrows. He didn't know how to respond. I shrugged and explained, "I broke a glass and she thought of it as bad behavior, I guess." I shrugged again.

"Oh, Pumpkin, I'm sure it was an accident. Mommy didn't mean to break it." He said. "An accident is not bad. And Mommy broke it by accident." And he kissed her and let her slip to the floor. As he does everyday he put his arms around me and kissed me hello.

Angel smiled and waited until we separated. "Mommy was bad." John and I shrugged again and we both seemed to know it was not something worth continuing to talk about. She would learn. And Angel too seemed happy enough to let it go.

While I was cleaning up after dinner, John gave all his attention to playing with Angel. I loved hearing her squeals. Our parenting skills seemed to be working just fine. We had a lovely child with a happy disposition. No need for Dr. Phil, thank you very much!

The days flew by filled with joy and happiness as we watched our daughter grow and give us the love all parents wish for. We were thankful for our precious child.

As wrapped up in motherhood as I was I still found time to work with the committee responsible for the craft booth at the up-coming lawn fete for Christ the King Church. Because I had no baby-sitter for Angel the group agreed to meet at our house. It was a Wednesday morning and Angel was helping by dusting the dining room furniture where we'd sit around the table discussing our plans. Of course she didn't know I'd already taken care of that task. But she liked to help and be complimented for it.

"I'm done, Mommy. How'd I do?"

"Darling it absolutely shines! Great job! Thank you so much." I picked her up and kissed her cheek. "Will you play quietly in the living room where I can see you during my meeting?" She nodded. "And will you not talk to Mommy unless you have to go to the bathroom?" I said smiling all the while. "I will Mommy; I promise."

"That's my girl." The doorbell rang. I put her down and sat her where she would be surrounded by toys to keep her busy.

Soon all committee members were sitting around the table, including Father Paul. We began with a prayer and at the end Angel called out, "Amen." Everyone laughed while looking at Angel. She smiled sweetly and went back to her playing. It was a long meeting and we accomplished so much. It was gratifying. I saw my company to the door. Fr. Paul was last out the door, "Thank you so much Jan for serving on the committee and for having us meet here. And what a blessed gift you have in Angel. It is hard to believe that she played quietly during that long meeting."

"Thank you Father, we know we are blessed. But just maybe the priest who baptized her had an influence." He grinned at the compliment. I assured him that I'd get those phone calls taken care of tomorrow.

I smiled at Angel, "You were such a good girl. So let's go to McDonald's for lunch. How does that sound?"

"Yay, Mommy!"

It was a quiet afternoon with Angel napping. I made pasta sauce for dinner. It was simmering on the stove. An easy meal so I had time to relax with a good book I'd found little time to enjoy. The reading and rest was short lived; Angel called the end of her nap. We took care of the after-nap rituals and we waited for our guy to come home.

John was late. He looked exhausted. He greeted Angel with the usual enthusiasm; but when he kissed me I knew he'd had a rough day. I poured him a glass of wine. All the while Angel kept trying to get his attention. "Angel, give Daddy a few minutes. He is very tired. He'll listen to you later."

"Let me hold her and pay attention; I could use a pleasant distraction. Okay Buttercup, what's up?"

"Mommy was bad today."

"Not again!" I thought. It was some time since we'd dealt with the "bad" word. I sat next to them to be a part of this new dilemma.

"Mommy was bad? How was she bad?" John asked.

"There was a man here today and Mommy was bad!"

My heart shriveled. What was this?

"What about this man, Angel? What did he do?" John tried not to rush the explanation.

"He touched Mommy's face."

"How did he do that?"

"He rubbed his hand on her face, like this," and she caressed John's face. John looked at me and I shrugged. Where was this going?

"Did he do anything else?"

"Yes!" He touched her on her sweater right there," and she pointed to his breasts. John looked at me again. Enough!

"Who was this man, Angel?"

"I don't know his name. He's the man from church." Oh my God! She meant Father Paul!

I couldn't think. John asked her what did this man do after he touched her. John couldn't really think any of this was true?!

"He went out the door. Mommy was bad."

"Okay, Sweetie, we'll talk about this later."

Somehow we got through dinner. I had time to think and I knew the explanation. John and I would laugh about it even though this would worry us about Angel. Thank God we trusted each other and would work together to help Angel.

Playtime with Daddy! Dishes! Finally bedtime for our little girl. I sat on the sofa waiting for John to finish reading a story. Finally I heard him coming down the stairs. I needed a hug. I needed comforting. John sat in the chair across from the sofa. What?!

"Well you've had plenty of time to come up with an explanation." he challenged.

"John, I have an explanation. And why are you sitting there instead of holding me. I'm the accused!"

"Yes, a three-year-old is an accuser! Come on Janice."

"You believe it? Wow!"

"Janice, a three-year-old is not so sophisticated as to dream up an adult scenario like she described. Unless, of course, you sit around all day watching The Young and the Ruthless while Angel hears and sees things no child should."

"Don't be ridiculous! So you believe it?"

"Janice, was a man here today? And if so- who?"

"I told you the lawn fete committee was meeting here because I couldn't leave Angel."

"Janice, there are no MEN on that committee. WAS there a man here today?"

"I thought we trusted each other, John. But yes, there was a man here. Fr. Paul! Hardly a womanizer!"

"Oh, no? You're right I don't believe he's a womanizer either." She let her breath out. Thank goodness.

"But I do think he could be interested in YOU! I've seen how he looks at you."

Janice could not believe what she was hearing. Her heart was pounding; soon it would fly right out of her chest.

"I might go over to the rectory and talk to Fr. Paul myself! Then we'll see!" John threatened.

Now Janice was angry. "Go! I want you to. If you're man enough to admit you were wrong. You have misjudged me; but worse yet you've misjudged a man of the cloth. GO!"

John grabbed his cars keys and ran out. She was alone. John had hurt her- badly. And she was extremely worried about Angel. They had to be a united front to sort out the reasons for these things Angel was dreaming up. After two hours of waiting she wondered what had happened to John.

Finally she heard him pull into the garage. He came in through the kitchen. When he saw her he hung his head. She hurried to him and held him in her arms. "Janice, I'm so sorry." She didn't say anything. She just waited. Then he began to hold her. He worried, "What are we going to do with Angel?"

"Let's first make things right with US." She answered. "What did Father Paul say? I have to know before I can face him again."

John explained, "He said that as he was leaving he put his hand on your shoulder and made the sign of the cross on your forehead. And Angel had seen him because she was standing next to you."

"And do you believe him?" John shook his head yes and held me tighter.

"Can you forgive me, Jan?" I kissed him. That was my answer. He asked, "What are we going to do about Angel?"

"I think we can still accept that she reported what she thought she saw. She's only a baby. But what worries me is this whole idea of 'bad' from her point of view. I don't want her sweetness to even consider anything bad."

She was our baby and we were still not objective about anything having to do with her. I think it was perfectly understandable that we would simply believe it would not happen again and we'd just get on with our life.

John apologized profusely in the days that followed. He repeatedly told me that he trusted me. But he still maintained that he reacted as he did because he couldn't believe a three-year-old could suspect and relate to such an adult behavior.

In the following weeks we were especially careful of our topics of conversation. But since there were no more "bad" days from Angel, we soon forgot about it and enjoyed our perfect child. The blessings derived from this difficult time for us led to a closeness between John and me that we hadn't known before. We were more romantic and our love-life flourished again.

Angel was developing more language skills, expanding her word knowledge, less baby talk and more complete sentences. Our child continued to grow right before our eyes. Days flew by and John and I tried to fill them to capacity. Continued joy and love. We said many prayers of thanksgiving for our perfect little girl.

Angel had been begging for a puppy, but we wanted to wait until she was a little bigger. An over-enthusiastic dog could knock her over, she was so small. One afternoon a dog from down the street was jumping up outside our fence, barking for Angel's attention. I didn't want her to be afraid of dogs so I waited to see what would happen. Before I could call to her she opened the gate and let the puppy in. She squealed with excitement as the puppy jumped up on her in his own excitement. She wasn't afraid and kept telling him, "Down! Down!" She threw Raggedy Ann and he chased wildly to retrieve it. He brought it back and dropped it in front of her. She recognized the game and they continued.

I decided that if I watched intently she could have some fun with him. And she'd learn how a dog behaved and how to handle it. If it got too rough I would go out and shoo the puppy away. And sure enough Angel learned an important lesson about dogs. They poop! And they didn't really care where. I didn't want her romping around in dog poop so I went out to clean it up. I took a shovel with me and a plastic bag as a container.

"Shoo, puppy," I called. And of course he thought I wanted to play too and he ran to me. I held the shovel out so he would stop, which he did. I moved toward the gate and shut him out. Angel ran to me, "Oh, Mommy, don't let him out. I want to play with the puppy."

"No, Angel, the puppy has to go to his house. His owner might be missing him."

"No, Mommy, I want him in our yard. I want to play with him."

"No, Darling, the puppy went home already. And it's time for your nap."

"Okay, Mommy." And like always Angel obeyed without question. She didn't whine or cry, like most children her age.

Soon she was smiling and asked, "Mommy sing that song that you always sing for my nap." I did and hummed quietly as I left the room which housed my perfect sleeping angel.

And I did the dirty duty and bagged the token Puppy had so generously given us.

Angel and I watched cartoons waiting for John to come home. I made chicken salad and set the table so there was not much more to do. We giggled and Angel would periodically jump up and kiss me. I reveled in the attention from our bundle of energy.

Angel heard the garage door swinging up before I did. She bolted off the sofa and ran to the door, "Daddy! Daddy!" He opened the door and she flew into his arms, showering him with kisses. He winked at me over her head as he planted a big kiss on her mouth.

"How's my Pumpkin?" She clung to him and said, "Mommy was bad today, Daddy."

My heart sank and John flinched. I sat down at the table unable to stand on legs that would not support me. "Careful, John." We had agreed the last time that if this came up again we would not jump to conclusions. We would listen, try to think it through and choreograph what we would do next. He shook his head in agreement. He pulled a chair from the table, sat and settled Angel in his lap.

"Okay, Sweetie. Tell me why you think Mommy was bad."

When I heard the word again my stomach lurched and I thought I might throw-up. I smiled at Angel as she looked at me like the executioner. "Tell Daddy, Honey."

"Oh, Daddy, the cutest puppy came into our yard today."

"How could he come in? Was the gate open?"

"No, Mommy let him in," she was looking at John and I shook my head 'no'.

"Then what happened?"

"Mommy didn't like the puppy. It was so cute, Daddy. She got the shovel and hit the puppy's head, three times. I counted. I can count to twenty-five. But she only hit him three times." She shook her head up and down. "I opened the gate so the puppy could run home. It was all bloody! Mommy said 'Good riddance.' What does that mean?"

"Why do you think Mommy hit the puppy?"

"Because he pooped in our yard. He didn't mean to."

John was quiet for a few moments. How to handle this. He looked at me and asked, "What do you say happened, Mommy?"

What! What was this? Witness for the accused? No, wait a minute I'm the accused. What did he want? The accused to give a full confession? Or maybe a plea deal? I stared at him in disbelief. He was supposed to explain to our **three-year-old** that it was hard to believe this story-at least!! Finally I answered, "What do you think happened, DADDY?"

He saw I was furious. "Okay, Pumpkin, Mommy and I will talk about this tonight and then tell you what we think, tomorrow. Okay?"

"Mommy was bad --but I'm hungry," our perfect little girl said.

We had dinner. John played with Angel until it was her bedtime. She asked me to put her to bed. I hugged her close and rubbed her back. None of this was her fault. She was too little to understand. And certainly neither John nor I knew how to explain it. After a story Angel fell asleep quickly. I found John sitting on the sofa. I sat beside him.

We both sighed at the same time. Well at least we were together on that!

John spoke first. "Why are you so angry, Jan?"

"Why? Why? This isn't a case of she said, Mommy said! This is our child who somehow lies—lies she should not be smart enough to create! And if you approach it as though we need to give an explanation for it, that it could have happened, Angel will continue. She needs to know that it didn't happen **and** it couldn't happen because her Mommy is incapable of the badness she proclaims. John, she needs first and foremost to know that her mother is **not** bad. I think that is our first step. We will probably need professional help to determine why Angel does **and** can create these stories. And we need help to know how to stop this from happening again."

"Really, Jan, Angel is just a baby. She is too little to know some of the things she claims she sees. It must come from somewhere in her world. What three-year-old knows what men do when they are attracted to a woman? Honestly?"

"Are you saying that her mother behaved like a woman who likes to be touched by a man other than her husband?"

"Well, she has to have seen it somewhere!"

I flew off the sofa! I realized that being angry wasn't going to help the situation-not help Angel.

"And has she seen me beat a puppy bloody? This 'bad' story differs completely from the first. In the first I was a hussy, cheating on my husband. In the second I am capable of violence and lacking in compassion. You see, John?"

"What exactly did happen with the puppy?"

"Your questions are revealing so much about your trust in me, John. You shouldn't even have to ask what happened. Angel didn't misconstrue what happened. She made it up."

"Come on, Jan, she's just a baby. There is something you must be doing to confuse her like that! And we definitely don't need **a professional** to find something wrong with Angel! She's just a baby and we are her parents. We'll take care of it!"

"How, John? By monitoring her mother for evidence of poor role-modeling?"

"Don't be ridiculous, Jan! I'll talk to Angel tomorrow night after supper. You worry too much or you wouldn't get so upset." He started up the stairs without a 'good night'.

I stopped him mid-way up. "Yes, John I am worried about Angel; but I am even more worried about what you are willing to believe about your wife. We need to support each other and, frankly, I don't see that happening from you. Angel is a child and can be brought up to be a trusting and loyal member of her family. You have disappointed and hurt me. I am not guilty but you certainly make me feel like you believe I am; or I am responsible for this problem. I am **not** and you are wrong if you suspect I am the source of her lies. These are lies and we should begin to address them as lies or if 'lies' is too harsh a word then as miss-truths. I'm finished so you can go on up to bed if you think you can sleep. I know I won't. You can deal with the one problem -that of our little girl. I'll be dealing with two—our daughter and my disloyal husband."

Tomorrow night Angel will be in another world of reference. Problems with children have to be addressed immediately. John, whether he realizes it or not, somehow thinks I am a catalyst for Angel's behaviors. I certainly am not but to tell the truth I am more frightened than I am worried. When will this end? John is not interested in how to help Angel. Our love should heal it all!? I pray he's right but I have little confidence in that happening.

The next night John and I were not speaking. After dinner John took Angel outside on the porch. They were there a long time but I did not interfere or even listen in. I felt sure I should have been there but John did not offer. So what he said, I don't know. Finally, near Angel's bedtime they came into the living room. Angel approached me, "I'm sorry, Mommy, about the puppy."

"I forgive you, Sweetheart. But I want to know why you told the puppy story."

She pretended to be distracted by the tassel hanging from one of the sofa pillows and simply said, "Because I didn't like to see the blood on the puppy," and she went to the corner to pull out some of her toys. I looked at John and he looked as though he couldn't believe what he had heard. He shrugged. Saying 'I'm sorry' did nothing to change her story. One for Angel. Zero for Daddy!

Life went on. John and I communicated as little as possible. Angel seemed completely unaffected by the coolness in her home. She loved me and she loved her father. I counted the days as they crawled by. Sixty seven days. A 'bad' day was about due. I know John looked upon the long time between her stories as a miracle cure. It's what he wanted and so he believed it!

The possibility of a 'bad' repeat was beginning to wear on my nerves. I tried not to be any different with Angel. She was only three. But the realization that she reported badness only in me and not her father or anyone else was disconcerting and something that needed to be brought to the surface if we were to solve this mystery. I was reasonably sure that a doctor or child psychologist could help us understand and find us a strategy for helping Angel to stop lying. John doesn't agree with me though; we both had to agree to pursue finding help. John spent most of the weekends with her, especially since we were at odds. No 'bad' was ever reported about her father. And we couldn't just wish away the level of sophistication in her reports. Why John did not wonder about these factors and feel, as

I did, that professional guidance was necessary for us to understand and how to deal with it, left me baffled. Was he so afraid there would be some suspicion about him and me that he refused to open up and ask for help. If not for our reputation but certainly to help our child.

Also eating away at me was the fact that my marriage might be falling apart. I am positive I cannot live with this masquerade of a marriage. My hands shook; I simply could not control them. I couldn't sleep. I was beginning to have difficulty getting through the day without breaking down. I have panic attacks where I can't breathe. I am so frightened. Was I somehow responsible for Angel's problem? I was beginning to doubt myself. It wasn't fair! I had to live with it. John did not! He was loved and not accused. When I told him that, he responded, "Now you're jealous! How much of this do **you** need as attention for you, instead of a little three-year-old? How can I give you attention when our baby needs me more? How much more of this can I take? Think of someone else besides yourself, Janice!"

I ran outside in the dark and vomited. The pains in my stomach were getting worse and more frequent. I'd lost 8 pounds over-night! Tomorrow was Sunday but I'm not going to Mass. I hated John at the moment. What peace can I find if I hate someone? His lack of trust was eating away at me.

And, oh, my daughter! She needs help and it won't come from her father's efforts to stop these stories she tells. But what can I do? I'm a mess. A professional will wonder about me too. I'm a real mess. I can't take much more of this.

Somehow I got through the weekend. It's Monday. Angel and I went shopping for a birthday card for Nana. We planned to drive to John's parents to celebrate with them. All the cousins would be there and Angel was very excited.

Angel found a pretty card covered with flowers and insisted we buy that one. Great! We walked to the cashier and stood in a short line to pay for the card. I handed her a twenty dollar bill. She bagged the card and gave me change for a five. She was talking all the while to another young clerk. She was distracted. "Oh," I said, "I gave you a twenty dollar bill.

"No, you gave me a five," she said. Another woman was standing right behind me waiting; and she told the cashier that she saw me hand her a twenty. I smiled at her.

"I'm sure she gave me a five, but I can have the manager check the register. It will show any mistakes."

"Please," I smiled to show I was not upset with her.

The manager appeared and the cashier related the circumstances. "Oh, yes; the register will clear up any mistake." The lady behind said again that she'd seen me give the cashier a twenty.

"You wouldn't believe how many times someone will display a scene to embarrass us, hoping to make money on the incident, the manager told us. I smiled and reminded him that a witness saw me hand her a twenty.

"Sometimes they will work in cahoots with one another. People pull all kinds of tricks. But yes, you did in deed give her a twenty according to the register. I am so sorry. Sara be more careful please," he emphasized. "Have a nice day ladies," as he walked away.

"Mommy, let me carry Nana's card."

"Okay, but be careful not to bend it. We don't want a wrinkled card for Nana."

We're waiting for John to come home from work. He opened the door and Angel ran to him. He picked her up and swung her around. She squealed as usual. He gathered her to him and questioned her. "Did my girl have a nice day?"

"Yes, Daddy. We bought a card for Nana. But, Daddy, Mommy was bad today.

I flew out of the kitchen and into the pantry. I told myself I didn't even care how I was bad. I didn't want to know. But I did. I stood close to the door and listened.

"Tell me about it Pumpkin." He sounded almost glad to hear I was guilty again.

"Mommy gave the lady who takes the money a five dollar and Mommy said she gave her a twenty dollar. I know a five on a dollar and I know a twenty on a dollar. It is a two o. The lady called a man and he came and told Mommy that she was trying to get too much money back. Mommy said it was a twenty and another lady said she saw Mommy give the girl a twenty two o. But she didn't see it. I did. It was five not a two o. Mommy and the other lady tried to get more money. The man said they were 'hoots'. What's a hoot, Daddy?"

"Don't worry about it, Angel. I'll talk to Mommy."

Oh sure he'd talk to me alright. His first question will be, "Why did it look like you tried to cheat?"

"Jan, come out and explain."

I rushed out and as I passed him I said, "There's nothing to explain. She told you how it was." I grabbed my purse and car keys.

"Come on Jan, I know it didn't happen that way!"

"So good of you." I left. I stopped at a liquor store and purchased a bottle of wine. I drove around, drawing gulps of the vino. I looked at the clock on the dash board. It read, 2:30 am. I went home and climbed the stairs to the guest room that was getting a lot of use lately. John opened his door and saw how drunk I was. "How are you going to be able to take care of Angel tomorrow?"

"You'd better plan to stay home." I closed the door and fell onto the bed, clothes and all.

The next morning I slept 'til eleven o'clock. I heard John talking to Angel. What does Mommy do after breakfast?"

She cleans up the kitchen. You better do it. Mommy's sick. She can't do it.

"Okay Angel. You go play in the living room. I'll clean the dishes."

"Mommy always scrubs the floor after the dishes. We don't want crumbs on our shoes and then walk on the rugs."

"Way to go, Baby!" Then I had a realization. Angel's stories always had information that actually was true. However, she twisted the information to reflect poorly on me. Something else a professional could help us understand. I curled up on the bed again. I couldn't think; I was so sick. Stupid of me to drink with my stomach the way it had been for weeks. I fell asleep. I woke up and it was 3:45pm. I showered and went down to the kitchen to prepare dinner.

John was reading the paper. "Well, it's about time. I have to go to the office and try to finish what I was supposed to do today. Don't plan dinner for me. I'll have take-out delivered to the office." He tossed the paper, grabbed his briefcase and left. Angel was dirty and was dragging along. She hadn't had a nap today.

"Hi, Sweetie. How does macaroni and cheese sound?"

"Yummy! Thank you, Mommy," and she wrapped her arms around my legs. I picked her up and we cuddled. All was good between us again--for now.

Since we'd just had a 'bad' day I figured I had a breather; the time between episodes was always several weeks. We left early a couple of days later to have our hair cut. Angel never complained like some children did because I allowed her to have her finger nails polished. She chose a gross shade of green. I stuck with the traditional red. We stopped at McDonald's, a part of the ritual. Driving home we were stopped at a red light. A teenager was stopped behind us. The light turned green-it took me a second to respond. The young man was very impatient and laid on his horn to prompt me. To reward his impatience I literally crawled through the intersection—not cool, but I was peeved. Our windows were down and as he passed us he shouted, "Asshole!" and flew his finger at me. It scared Angel and I tried to calm her down. "That was rude!" She agreed, "Yes it was!"

"Angel, don't ever say that word."

"Okay, Mommy."

"That word hurts people's feelings and makes them feel so sad. You don't want to do that." Take a chance here, Janice. "Another thing that hurts someone is if you tell something that isn't true. Remember that, Baby." "Okay, Mommy, I will. I promise. What is truth, Mommy?"

"Truth is telling only things that really happened. No pretend. I hope you always tell the truth."

"I will."

"Good girl. Let's forget that boy and what he said; because we don't say bad words. It's isn't nice." Lesson #1? It's a start. Real learning comes with applying what we 'know'. We'll see if Angel can put this together and think before presenting fabrications. She's only three; it might take a while.

Pork chops! And apple sauce. Baked potato! I wanted a really delicious dinner tonight. I set the table in the dining room. With the oven on it was too uncomfortable to eat in the kitchen. Homemade lemonade was a favorite for all three of us. I was starting to breathe more comfortably—no 'bad' stories. I think John was more relaxed too.

He came into the kitchen and tossed his jacket and briefcase on a chair he'd pulled out from the table. "H-m-m, eating formal are we?" He smiled. I returned it. I was busy at the stove. "Where's my Buttercup?" We heard a muffled response.

"I'm hiding. Come look for me."

John looked in the closet. No Angel. We heard her giggle. John looked behind the pillows on the sofa. "No Angel."

"Daddy, you are so silly. I'm behind the sofa."

John sneaked up and kneeled on the sofa. He surprised her; she was expecting him to stand at the end and catch her. Before she realized what happened he grabbed her and swung her up and over the sofa to the floor. She giggled, a really sweet sound. Love mixed with excitement. Her father pulled her up in an embrace and they hugged like two bears on the Animal Planet. She was breathless. "Daddy, I wish you could stay home all day."

"Me too, Sweetie; me too! I love you Pumpkin."

Angel sighed. "Mommy was bad today, Daddy." Oh, everything seemed too perfect to warrant a 'bad'!

"Try to distract her, John. Do something to steer her away from what's to come."

But John said, "What happened today, Angel?"

What was he doing?! It was almost as though he were building a case---against me! "Oh, God, please!" There was no way out for me. "Help me please!"

"A boy honked his horn at Mommy and she called him a bad word."

"What word, Angel?"

"I can't say it. Mommy told me not to say it. It is a bad word."

"You can whisper it in my ear." "Okay." She said as she looked at me. She knew she was disobeying me, something she never did. John, come on! This is not the way to handle it!

"Okay," and she said it. I could hear and she'd said it."

"Janice, you are taking this too far. She's three!"

"**I'm** taking this too far. What are you trying to tell me, John? You blame me. Do you know how idiotic that is?"

John shouted, "You are doing something, Jan. It never happens around me. I want to trust you, but I can't anymore. What are you doing to our little girl? I love you, but we have to face the fact that there is something happening to you. You are not well. You have to get help, Jan. I'll help you. I'll call the AMA tomorrow and ask for a recommended top-notch doctor who can help you. You'll be alright again, Jan." He stared at me. As he stood there holding my precious child I crumbled to the floor. I wanted to die!

He carried me up to the guest room and helped me to the bed. He removed my shoes and pulled the coverlet up to my chest. He placed my arms on top of my body. "Sh-sh," and he kissed my forehead. I might as well have been catatonic. I couldn't move; I couldn't talk; I couldn't think!

Next thing I knew John was waking me up. "I have to go into the office for a couple of hours," he said. "You'll have to watch Angel. I've dressed and fed her. She's playing in the toy corner downstairs."

"I can take care of her. There is nothing wrong with me, John. I'm just sick from what you think of me." And I started down the stairs.

John followed and left for work. The kitchen was left just as it was when I collapsed. I guess I'm well enough to do the grunt work. I ignored it and called my best friend, Anna. She had just returned from Europe where she was on a photography stint. She took beautiful photos and was our wedding photographer as her wedding gift to us. We'd been friends since college days. I needed to talk with someone I could trust.

Anna greeted us at the door with a hug for me and a smooch for Angel. "Come on in," she invited. "Coffee? Milk?" She looked to Angel.

"I want chocolate milk please." We laughed at her boldness.

"Well, I'll tell you what. I have white milk but I also have some chocolate in a bottle. How about mixing them together?" Anna offered. Angel shook her head yes.

"Can I watch cartoons?"

"Absolutely! I'll put your chocolate milk in a sippy cup so we don't have to worry about spilling. How does that sound?"

Simultaneously, I said great and Angel shook her head vigorously.

After settling Angel in on the sofa I told Anna I needed to talk. She took the cue and suggested we could talk privately in the family room and still see Angel.

I started at the beginning and had a few break-downs along the way. Anna listened compassionately but watched Angel to see if she could possibly hear. When I described how emotional I was and how I was beginning to question if I was responsible for Angel's stories, Anna suggested we put Angel up in Anna's guest room with a TV.

"Yes, and most likely she would fall asleep." I said.

Anna stated that I needed to be as open as I wanted to be and Angel didn't need to be a part of that. I agreed. We settled Angel down and turned on the cartoon channel. She was perfectly content.

Anna listened to me for over an hour. It felt so good to get it off my chest.

"I have every confidence that you are not responsible for Angel's stories. I agree she needs help. What is wrong with John, thinking you are capable of all those things?"

"Thanks, Anna, I needed to hear someone agree with me."

"How about some more coffee? I'll make a new pot."

"Okay but while you're doing that I'll go up and see how Angel's doing. While I'm up there I'll use your bathroom."

"Of course." Jan could smell the ground coffee and it was comforting.

Angel had fallen asleep just as Jan had thought she would. She used the bathroom and admired the color schemes Anna put together and the beautiful photos along the wall of the short hall.

As she entered the kitchen Anna looked up, "Sit down, Jan. And now I want you to listen to me." Jan sat and sipped her coffee.

"Jan, I definitely agree and support your wisdom in what to do to help Angel. But I do worry about you." Jan nodded but she felt less comfortable than she had two sentences ago. "You are a mess—sorry, friend. You're nothing but a skeleton. Your nerves are shot. Trembling and near tears all afternoon. I think John is right—wait a minute—hear me out. He's right that doctors or specialists who diagnose Angel's problem will examine your emotional stability. They might want help for you before they'll counsel her. You have to pull yourself together which may mean counseling for you and that which is troubling you will impact their decisions as to what to do for her."

Jan was stunned! How did this happen? I'm not to blame but I **am** to blame! What do I do next. I **know** I was stable before all this. Yes, physically I may need help. But what had been the cause? I was hurt with Anna's analysis. I am innocent. I'm a good mother. I'm not the kind of person my own daughter thinks I am. And John was an asshole—there!

I'd said it. Maybe I am that person. I'd always thought I was a good woman. Maybe I'd only been fooling myself.

Jan couldn't even answer Anna. She merely stood, pushed her chair back under the table. Without a word she went upstairs, claimed her baby and grabbed her purse and went out the front door. All the while Anna tried to reason with her. "Jan, don't leave. I was just trying to help you see what might come next when you engage a doctor to help Angel." Angel was crying because her mother was sobbing. She'd come here hoping to find someone to take her side, not John's. Her life was over. On the drive home she told herself that maybe she was the instigator and just didn't see it because she couldn't face the fact that it was her. She'd give Angel to John, a much more stable parent, and disappear from their lives. She'd put Angel first on her present priority list. That's why she had to absent herself from their lives. She pulled into their driveway and John's car was there. Anna must have called John and he came home to make sure Angel was okay. Angel got out of the car and John scooped her up into his arms.

"What happened?" asked John

"It's all taken care of John, I'm leaving."

"You can't go like this, Jan.

"Oh, you'll get the kitchen cleaned up, John. Maybe you could hire a cleaning lady."

"I don't mean that, Jan. I don't want you to go. I'll get help for your problems. I told you that." All the while Angel sat in the corner with her toys.

Just then the doorbell rang. "Let it go, Jan. We're into too much right now to deal with anyone." "Okay," she mumbled.

Very loud banging was followed by an order! "Open the door! Police!" Another round of banging. John looked at Jan. She returned the look with wide frightened eyes. They must have been shouting louder than she thought!

John opened the door. The two policemen entered as though it made the difference between life and death. Angel stared from her corner but she didn't act frightened.

"Officers, yes, my wife and I were arguing but we didn't know we were so loud that the neighbors would call the police!

The taller of the two officers stated, unfeelingly, "Your neighbors didn't call us. A woman," and he referred to his notepad, "Anna Duggan did."

Jan looked shocked, why would she call the police? Maybe she was afraid I was so upset that she wanted to make sure we got home safely. Jan, bewildered, shook her head, not understanding.

"Are you Janice Avery?" She nodded yes to the officer, even more bewildered. "We need to talk to you, Mrs. Avery."

"About what?" she asked.

"Not in front of the child." The room began spinning for Janice; her balance a worry; but she led them to the family room and pointed to chairs. They all sat. John could see Angel playing from his vantage point.

"A diamond ring owned by Anna Duggan went missing today after your visit to her home."

"Oh, that ring is beautiful!" Jan said. "She must be sick to find it missing; it meant so much to her. Given her by her grandmother."

"Then you know the ring and have seen it?" the officer asked.

Only the tall officer spoke; the second took notes.

"Did you see the ring today?"

"No. I imagine she keeps it in a safe or something."

"Well Mrs. Duggan says the ring was there before you arrived and was gone after you left."

All the blood left Jan's face, "Sh —She thinks I took it? No, no, we're best friends. She knows I'd never steal anything. Did she **say** she thought I took it?"

"No, she didn't say that, but—"

Angel interrupted from the other room, "Mommy was bad today, Daddy. When she came upstairs to wake me up— she didn't know I was already awake and she went into Aunt Anna's bedroom and took the ring that was on the dresser. When she came out she called me to hurry because we were going home. When we went downstairs she grabbed her purse and put the ring in it. Mommy was bad."

Jan was astounded. "I did not go into Anna's bedroom or take her ring. I did not!"

"One way to find out," the officer said. "Where's your purse, Mrs. Avery?"

Jan was so confused she thought, "Um—she looked around. "Oh, I know. I was so upset that I left it in the car."

"I'll get it," John said.

"No, Officer Moody will get it." And the other officer left to get the purse.

By this time Angel was in the thick of things. John told her to go back to her toys. "Yes, Daddy."

Officer Moody handed the tall officer Jan's purse. Now they'd see she thought. The contents of her purse were dumped on the officer's hanky spread on the floor.

There was the diamond ring, sparkly and lovely. Jan gasped and fainted. The next thing she knew she was lying on the sofa and John was cooling her face with a wet washcloth. The officer was talking to Anna, on the phone, promising to return the ring after it was cataloged.

"Mrs. Avery, you'll have to come with me to headquarters for questioning. You will not have to stay. Your husband can come with us and be present for your questioning. Mrs. Duggan has not decided whether or not to press charges."

Mary Jane Casey Lane

She was numb. She looked at John and said, "What about Angel?"

John said he would call a babysitter they'd hired a few times and then come to be with her.

The next few hours were very difficult for Jan. She felt like a robot going through the motions that were not real. She went home with John.

He looked at her. "Should I stay home tomorrow and help you get through the day? Officer Emanuel said we probably won't hear anything tomorrow."

"No," she answered, "I'll be fine. But John, when the officers' came to the house neither one of them said the ring was on the dresser. You certainly wouldn't know it. I didn't know it; I never went into Anna's room. How come Angel knew it was on the dresser?"

John sighed, "I don't remember if she said dresser or not. Besides how would she be able to reach it? She couldn't, Jan."

Jan thought, "Now I have my answer. No support from any quarter! What's the use?!"

The next day was a long one. It was hot and muggy and John had loosened his tie and discarded his jacket. The house was hot; why hadn't Jan turned on the AC? He didn't have a flying bullet in the form of a little girl fly into his arms? "Angel, where are you?"

126

She called out from the den, "I'm playing in a tent house under your desk."

Sure enough she had Raggedy and Teddy under his desk. "Where's Mommy?"

"I don't know. She didn't even call me for my nap. And I had to eat poleons. But they're only crackers for real."

"Okay, keep playing. I'll go look for Mommy. I'll tell you when I find her."

"Okay, Daddy."

John checked the upstairs, even the attic; all the while calling her name. He decided to check the closets, as foolish as that was. She wouldn't be in a closet. He was getting nervous; maybe she'd left, but, no, her car was parked outside. Maybe she walked somewhere. He checked all the downstairs without calling her name; he didn't want to upset Angel. Where else could she be. Maybe the basement. A chill went through his body. Not what he was thinking, "**please**!" He descended slowly. He reached the bottom. A shadow was all he saw and he knew; so he turned and went back up to the kitchen. He called 911.

At the wake he stood by the casket talking to Fr. Paul. "How does the church feel about suicide, Father. Does she automatically go to Hell?"

Angel, standing next to her father looked up, startled by his question.

The mass finally ended all the commotion in their lives and John took Angel home for an afternoon nap. He tucked her in, hugged her and kissed her cheek.

She looked up at him.

She didn't speak right away.

Finally she said, "You were bad today, Daddy!"

A BOY
A HERO
AND
MISS
JENNINGS

A Short Story
By
Mary Jane Casey Lane

This is the day I look forward to every year. The first day of school; the kick-off of the game, setting the tone for my classroom and my students, their first impression of me, their new teacher. My job begins even before the bell rings, introducing the start of the new year. It is my job to capture an excitement and instill it in my students. After a couple of weeks of school, discipline was not much of a problem for me. My students were usually happy because of the mutual respect I found important to exhibit and establish. Expectations and routines were pretty much already ingrained. I take my work very seriously and find teaching very rewarding. We had to quickly get to the place where we all accept what is expected of us.

The first day of school! I was as excited as my students at the ringing of the school bell. They usually came in shy and quiet. They smiled at me, sizing me up. My first assignment-measure up. It was a day that set the tone for the year. And I was nervous! "Really, Sherri? This is not Kindergarten! You've done this before," I chastised myself. I loved to watch them as they chose their desks, all empty, and up for grabs. I'd smile when a previous stake on a desk was abandoned because a friend entered the room, calling for a plan to sit together. And soon some brave soul would ask, "Will we have assigned seats?"

"Not as long as I won't find it necessary. I think you are old enough to make that decision and still do the job of being a good student." Whoa! Everyone looked from one face to another. One, more loquacious boy, (and it was almost always a boy) piped up, "Cool!" As he looked around to decide what other boy would be rewarded a desk next to him. And of course, the scene was complicated when a neighborhood 'gang' called for a group conference before choosing. Interesting negotiations when a desired desk was already claimed.

Sixth grade girls being sixth grade girls, changed best friends almost daily, so their selection went without much ado.

I loved the school building, itself. It was old. Long windows, large classrooms. But the feature that always fascinated me, was an old-fashioned 'cloak room' (like back in my day) separated from the classroom by a wall, something like a closet, which had a doorway directly into the classroom itself, one could walk in or out of the classroom without going into the hall, actually leaving the room; but a perfect place to goof off or other more imaginative mischief where the teacher couldn't see. Sometimes it served as a place for settling disputes, where they needn't fear being seen by me.

Sometimes being a teacher means being creative. It's called the 'art' of teaching. One given was that the door to the cloak room would always remain open. Yet the door was at the end of the cloak room meaning everything, and everybody, in there was invisible to me. To check someone or some activity in the cloak room I'd have to interrupt what I was doing and actually enter it to see the scenario within. And that proved very tempting for all varieties of assignations. One afternoon after a long day I studied for a solution to the unguarded area. I thought, "Think outside the box, Sherri." An idea surfaced. The solution was better than the proverbial 'eyes in the back of the head.'

Next morning the kids 'oohed' and 'ahed'. A full length mirror adorned the door at the end of the coat room and the teacher's desk had been moved, kitty-corner to it. And that solved that problem. How? Everything in the coat room was reflected in the mirror which I could see from my desk. That day I was asked to explain the mirror. "Well, when you guys come in you can check yourselves out. I know you want to look good." I nonchalantly stated. Very important for most sixth grade girls.

I waited patiently to try out my brilliant solution. Finally I saw two boys in the cloak room beginning to wrestle around. Now was my opportunity, "Joe and Kevin, stop fooling around and get to your seats." I could see their reaction and

Kevin asked, "How did she know it was us?" Joe shrugged his shoulders. Now sixth graders are pretty smart but no one ever figured it out, either that year or later years. And if they did, all the better! They'd have to be more secretive for mischief. It narrowed the possibilities considerably. Yes!

Most of my students had attended this school for most of their school years. But every year there would be a new-comer, arriving on the first day or sometime during the year. On my class list I saw a new boy, Richard Collins, better known as Rick. Rick was living in a Foster home, had moved in during the summer; and he had made a few friends before school started. On this first day he was surrounded by three or four boys, some just curious about him. I walked over to the group and welcomed him. He looked at me then dismissed me with his body language. "What a strange reception," I thought. "Not interested in this new teacher or what she might think of him. In-different. 'So you're the teacher. So?' Oh, well, I'll give him some space, for now."

Over the first few opening days of school I was busy getting to know all the children and establishing the environment for learning. I did, however, notice that Rick never made eye-contact with me. Never raised his hand. Never tried to get my attention. Never asked anything of me. I was concerned but to be honest, I was baffled. I'd never had a student quite like Rick. "What do I really know about a 'private' person, especially a twelve-year-old?" I frowned.

The second week of school, as in years past, I scheduled a parents' meeting to get acquainted and share my expectations for their child and for them. Usually I closed the meeting with some levity, "I promise not to believe everything that happens at home if you promise not to believe everything that happens at school."

After the meeting Rick's Foster mother asked for a conference. We settled on a date. I was sure I'd learn some things to help me in working with Rick. I'd pay closer attention to Rick, his interactions with the other kids, his attention span, his initiative, his work habits and motivation. Too soon to make any conclusive observations on my part. But I was really interested to know what his Foster mom thought; how he acted at home. I knew nothing of his history. While I was comfortable with the positive relationships I was developing with most of the kids, I knew, that generally my efforts were paying off. A few had been won over immediately while others needed more assurance that this classroom was a safe place where they were wanted and respected. And a place where they could learn without fear of their efforts leading to loss of respect and/or dignity. Rick? Nothing!

Finally the day of the conference with Mrs. Schwartz. Rick did not exhibit any anxiety about our meeting. Mrs. Schwartz said Rick had been with her family since the end of July. Her own two boys were in high school and first year college and the three boys were fine with each other during the summer; as well as Rick having made friends with a couple of boys in the neighborhood, one in this class and the other in another sixth grade. I confirmed that the two still seemed close in class as well. I was happy that Rick had this friend to help him adjust to a new school. "Mrs. Schwartz, have you observed a kind of indifference in Rick?" I asked.

She smiled and replied, "Toward me, yes," she replied. "He is fine with my husband and the boys."

"Do you know why I am having trouble reaching him?"

Again she smiled, a sad smile that seemed a way of comforting me, "It's because you are a woman."

"What?" I puzzled.

"You see Rick's father murdered his mother!" I gasped. This was a first for me.

"But wouldn't you think he'd miss her and crave female attention? Maybe not at first but eventually?" I challenged.

"I guess, I don't know." She sighed. "He was taken out of his home because his father was imprisoned. He confessed and will be tried for murder."

I shook my head. How awful for Rick! I shared that his learning seems to have been intact despite his emotional upheaval. "His behavior is not a concern to me at this time. What bothers me most is his indifference to me, to my expectations for learning and rules of behavior. I do suspect that he has his own high standards for his work, and appropriate behavior is self- imposed so he and I have no differences in those departments. I think he must have been an outstanding student before this horrendous event in his life. I don't want indifference affecting his work. So, we'll see where this goes. Is there anything you want from me or anything I can do to help you?"

"No." she said, "and thank you, Miss Jennings."

"You're welcome and we'll keep in touch."

(It's amazing how children learn to cope with tragedies in their lives.)

Soon we're rolling right along; no big problems getting in the way of learning. The kids are a joy. We all laugh often at some humorous thing that happens in our own little world in the classroom with the 'cloak room'. One day when we were giggling about something or other, I cautioned the children, the whole class chuckling, "We'd better not laugh. If somebody is walking by they'll think we like school!" And then we really laughed.

Rick joined in but not with the usual abandon of the other kids. I tried every day to give him some one-on-one banter or an account of the work he presented. On occasion he took a quick peek at my face, but still not eye to eye. I had absolutely no idea if he liked me or just tolerated me. I suspect that if I suddenly, with no warning, was taken from my position that he'd accept my disappearance with little regard. What was with this kid?! He didn't fit into any of the norms! No question he was a very private individual in our relationship. He made friends easily with the boys in class. Actually Rick was popular with the boys. They often gathered around his desk. I recognized that he could be a leader. I saw no other behaviors questionable to me. He was generally positive in only those things in which he chose to invest. He accepted that I made the choices for his learning. I did notice that girls never seemed to appear in his line of vision. He never interacted with them or bothered them. It's like this was an all-boys school. Girls didn't exist as far as Rick was concerned. "Give him more time, Sherri," I told myself. He was being counseled through the Foster Parent Program. As of yet there had been no sharing of their reports.

Fall was winding down. Football was in the air. Memorized stats amazed me. The boys rattled them off. If I could just interest them in the same way about long division I'd be an instant candidate for the Teachers' Hall of

Fame! Such was the world of elementary school. Teachers trying to stay ahead of the kids and making a difference. It was our heritage, leaving a mark on one little spot in the world. How I love this work! It is my world!

After all the years I'd invested you'd think I'd have heard it all. One morning before the bell the children were unpacking backpacks and catching up with each other. A boy, named Jerry, came to my desk. "You know what Miss Jennings?"

"What?"

"I wrote a letter to my uncle and told him all about you and he said he'd like to meet you."

The school Marm, at her age, entertained any potential suitor. "Oh, and where does your uncle live?"

"Well, right now he's in prison." D-d-d he say prison? Is this the way a balloon felt when you popped it with a pin?

Speaking about unexpected and humorous stories in every teacher's storybook- one Christmas season I asked if anyone could tell us the story of Christmas? (This was before all the fuss about religion in school dictated.) A boy raised his hand. "You're on." I said.

"Well Joseph and Mary got to Bethlehem and Mary's water broke!" I had to go home and ask my mother what 'Mary's water broke' meant. Not really, but kids know things now we'd never known as kids ourselves.

Another big part of being a teacher was the amusing excuses we'd get for unfinished home work. I'd call the offenders one at a time to come to my desk for a private explanation. Bubba (his nickname), a carrot top charmer explained, "My mother was very upset last night. So I couldn't finish my homework. You see she's going through the change of life!" Careful Miss Jennings; you' re heading in that direction. Oh, well. What's a boy to do?

I mentioned that Rick never would admit the existence of girls in the room. But one day a girl ventured to his desk and something went off in Rick's head. He'd never had a discipline issue. It was as though there wasn't anything in the world that was worth the effort or his attention. The girl's name was Cindy Huuefisch. It appeared she was nagging him about something. At first he ignored her, at which, she doubled back with another comment that I couldn't hear. But I could see how it affected Rick. He actually looked at her! "Get out of here 'ugface', a play on her last name created by a classmate and adopted by one and all, even the girls. This name-calling was presenting itself as a problem for me. Her mother called me about Cindy being harassed by the name-calling. I talked to the class about how hurtful name-calling can be and I forbad any further use of it. The problem with trying to control it was hampered by Cindy's imposing herself where she wasn't welcome. She moved from group to group and her contributions were usually negative. Most did not like her and I found Cindy to be that which they accused her of. She injected herself without being invited and would try to control the discussion. She'd make hurtful comments, almost as though she didn't realize she was hurting anyone. When she was caught in her own web, Cindy turned to tears, some I suspect were honest as well as some for theatrical effect. She was not well-liked. And I understood it. Very difficult. I'd talked with Cindy about this social problem and her contribution to it. She was lonely; that was clear. I tried creating activities where she'd have to work with classmates. She seldom completed a task she had volunteered to do and it reflected poorly on the group's presentation and grade for the project.

"Cindy, you have to be a friend to have a friend," I suggested. She'd improved somewhat over the year but needed to mature for better control and commitment.

Back to Rick and his outburst. I talked to him. He was not disrespectful but he wouldn't budge from his position. "I don't like her. She won't leave me alone," all said without looking at me.

"But knowing you are being hurtful doesn't bother you?" I pleaded.

"Nope!"

Irreversible! "She's crazy!" he pronounced. The problem of one child's reaction to the other child's problem. A huge sigh was heard from his teacher. Rick had never interacted in this way. He never would allow investing himself that much. He sat down. It was over. Whenever something was over for him, it was over! He'd simply go back to what he had been doing. You were dismissed. If only Cindy would realize that.

I felt certain Rick didn't think all women were 'no good'. He was only using anger to battle the opposing forces within him. He was afraid, having no mother and no father, so he dismissed any true emotions. He was uncertain of where and with whom he would live. Might as well dismiss anything he decided to; just as the world had dismissed him. Who could be trusted? He'd trusted his mother until he heard she was 'no good.' And who told him that? His father!

Autumn- football! For the first time Rick was animated, not for my benefit, however. He was a very excited fan of the Green Bay Packers and loved Bart Starr, his hero. It did my heart good to see Rick so enthusiastic and smiling as a group of boys had gathered during a 15 minute Free Time granted on most days. The others would listen to Rick because he could practically re-enact the whole game. He was the go-to man for stats and replays descriptions. But true to himself he didn't mix his enthusiasm with expected behaviors in class time. He was obedient. He was determined not to rock my boat; it was a ploy for control. It worked! So far! I wasn't giving up.

During another free time, however, I suddenly realized that Rick was telling the boys about his dad being in prison. I strolled over and listened in. He wasn't threatened by my presence. "Why is your dad in prison?" The big question was finally asked. They'd all wanted to know but didn't know how to broach the question. "Did I only imagine it or did each one of us literally lean into Rick so as not to miss his answer?" I thought.

"He shot my mother and killed her." GASP! Heard around the assembled group. Sympathizing I said, "How awful for you, Rick!"

His response, "No, she deserved it! My dad said she was no good and now he's in prison. My mother was no good." So matter-of-fact.

My heart ached for the boy. He had to side with his only living parent. And probably soon there would be no one-his family had disappeared.

Now I understood. His mother was 'no good'. So all women were no good. Now I knew I had to work at turning that around. But how? A solution had to present itself. "Think, girl."

And I got it! I wrote the letter over and over until I got it just right. At least I hoped so. I told what a big fan Rick was. I explained how excited Rick would be to hear from him and how I hoped he could send Rick some team souvenir. I addressed the envelope, "Green Bay Packers, Att. Bart Starr" and put it in the mail.

It was weeks but still football season. I would be so disappointed if the letter was ignored. I had explained that I was trying to reach a boy in my class and it wasn't happening. I didn't share any of Rick's story. I couldn't. That would be unprofessional and illegal. Finally an envelope, thick and bulky, was in my mail box. Return address: Bart Starr. I was so excited. There were pennants, badges, and (the biggy!) an autographed picture of Bart Starr with a special message to Rick! I'd tell Rick I had a friend who worked for the team and had asked him to do this for Rick, because I knew it would mean a lot to him.

Rick and the boys sat together and enjoyed the moment, but none as much as I. I did not disturb the party. This was for Rick. Someone loved him. Me! And it was a privilege to watch his joy.

Just before dismissal Rick came to my desk. He looked me right in the eye and said, "Thank you, Miss Jennings." And you know what he did?

He smiled!

I admit that neither Bart Starr nor I had changed forever Rick's opinion of the female persuasion. But he looked at me!!

In Bart Starr's letter to me he suggested that perhaps he and Rick could help me to love football too. It didn't happen that way; I learned to sometimes **like** football. But then after football season Rick didn't look at me very often. Hey, we'd fought the good fight; and we may not have won the war, but we did win the battle.

Hopefully we'd succeeded more than we thought! Perhaps we should leave Rick's world the way he creates it to survive. He is smart and I'm sure he'll succeed one day in trusting the real world; and feel no need to shut it off from himself. Then he will have won the war.

HAPPY SUMMER VACATION!!

I never saw Rick again after sixth grade.

BART STARR
Green Bay Packers 1956-1971

Pro-Football Hall of Fame 1977
Only Quarterback to lead team to 5 Championships
1961 1962 1965 1966 1967

THE LETTER

A Short Story
By
Mary Jane Casey Lane

The envelope read:

Cab Brickers   Stamp
New Orleans, Orleans Parish Louisiana   1825

     Newt Brickers
     Moreauxville, Aroyelles Parish Louisiana

Son,

I think you receev this letter. I hope. I meet a man here who work mail delivery - important man. He promis this git to you Moreauxville fast. I am settled here. We live more better than how we liv beefor. You git letter. Someone bring you to Baton Rouge or you walk. It a long way to walk, but do if you half to. Ther you go to mail place. Tell them Mr. Fayette pik you up. Do not go away from ther even all nite. Mr. Fayette go ther all Fridays and come to where I am- New Orleans—on Saterday. Go with him. I be ther waytin' for you. God be good for us, no? I sory leav you behin. Had to. I tel l you Y when you git heer.

                                          Cab – Fathur

Sal read the letter over and over. (You should know his real name is Newt.) He knew his father had not wanted to leave without him. Sal knew his father was a good man, that he'd gone to school for one day and then left to work beside Sal's grandmother to help the family. They had a square of land on which they planted and cared for in order to feed themselves. It was a job for them but they were not treated well or paid well. They did what they had to do; just as Sal's father had done what he had to do to preserve his dignity and to feed Sal's family. Sal knew his father would not just leave them behind. But it was so long since they'd heard from him. Sal carried many messages from his family members. At Moreauxville his father had worked the ovens for making bricks. And then one night he disappeared and regretfully left his kin behind. All those left behind felt with certainty that Cab (his real name; he joked that his name sounded like 'cake' but not as sweet) left only to protect them somehow. Sal was determined to do what his father had instructed by way of the letter.

No ride to Baton Rouge, so he walked. He sat down beside the dirt road to rest and read the letter yet one more time. His father was a dignified and intelligent man; one who saw between the lines of life and learned from it. He provided Sal more than just food to eat. He also gave him food for thought. Sal thought, "Father saw beauty where other men did not." He possessed common sense where others were tunnel-visioned and had often made fools of themselves as the consequence. He spoke as a learned man, which he was, though deprived of formal education. Sal went to school at the plantation. His father claimed that permission for Sal's formal learning made his grueling work and conditions bearable. Fortunately Father held hard work performance in high esteem. And Sal loved school. It was held every morning in the manor school room, with instruction from Miss Jennings, a strict but graceful woman who sparked curiosity in her students. Sal's was a dynamite spark. "You will make something of yourself one day, Newt. Put that in your head and your heart and never let it go. You are special!" praised his teacher. That was something Sal believed even though he was humble about most things-and definitely that! It warmed his father's heart and made him work harder which his employer noted and took advantage of.

Every night Sal sat with his weary father and taught him what he could. Cab was a quick learner but, exhausted, would drop off to sleep during his fractured lessons. Consequently he'd never learned to read well or write well. "But someday," promised his son. Cab Brickers could out-smart a man when he put his mind to it. But he held no prejudice toward coloreds or whites for that matter. He expressed himself and understood like a learned man and appeared to most as such. He felt no superiority over any man. He was respectful of women and never gazed too long on them, except Mama of course.

But what Sal loved most about his father was the way he saw and reflected on beauty that others didn't even see was there. At a still moment in the middle of the woods circling the farm land or surrounded by open fields that welcomed every wildflower and bird known to man, he would look up, close his eyes and spout thoughts that caressed the heart and made the hairs on your arms stand up. His words were a treasure to behold. Once Sal asked him if he could write down his words on paper. Cab smiled shyly and said, "I 'spect it wouldn't hurt if you left my name off it. A man can't be too uppity!" So that night Sal wrote his father's words:

"In these woods covered by the good Lord's
firmament I pray these words,

I know who I am
I know what I am
Help me, Lord, to be more than I am

Sal promised himself that one day he will publish his father's thoughts, now that he was given permission to write them down, anonymously of course. Thus the start of the biography of Cab Brickers. Sal wondered what his real last name was; Brickers was assigned by the boss man at Moreauxville. Sal loved his father and wanted to emulate him; he wanted to grow to be the man his father was.

"Gosh, how long have I been sitting here?!" he realized. "I'll have to put down for sleeping soon before the sun goes down." He got to his feet, took a drink from his canteen and looked forward. Not too far down the road Sal saw a boy leaning against the gate closing off the path to a plantation manor. The manor sat back and under several large trees, making it appear cool and inviting. Was the boy going in or coming out, Sal wondered.

As Sal neared the boy and the gate it was obvious the boy was poor and raggedy; that saddened Sal. He, as his father had instilled in him, tried to learn the heart of another human being; then, and only then, do his judging. Cab warned Sal to never judge a man by his cover, visible or invisible. "Especially," Cab admitted sadly, "a colored man." Because they were not permitted to think for themselves.

The boy by the gate, who too had been taught by his father, eyed Sal cautiously. "This is a boy who doesn't trust." Sal thought.

"Hey," Sal entered into conversation.

"Hey," the boy returned.

"What are you doing here at the gate? Do you live here?" Sal asked.

"F-f-f," the sound escaped the boy's mouth as he rolled his eyes. "Look at me. Sure, I live here. Are you stupid, boy?" He decided to drop the attitude. It never accomplished anything anyway. "Nah! I'm waiting for my Pap. He went to the door looking for work. Someone on the road told us there was a widder here whose husband died and all the farm hands, whites and coloreds alike took off, leavin' no one to farm her land. I reckon there's not much hope she'd hire the likes of us; we'd probably scare the bee-jesus outta' her. I hope she does though. Pap thinks she may hire him to work a small garden, enough to keep 'em eatin'. 'Sides we haven't et for two days save some nuts we found on the ground back," and he pointed down the road from which Sal had just come. "And most people are afeared of us like we're gonna' kill 'em or somin'. Stupid! It's more likely they'd kill us!"

Sal stood there staring at the dirty and disheveled boy. He admired his spunk.

"Watcha' lookin' at? I ain't afeared of you!" he punctuated his strength.

Sal retorted, "I hope not! I'm not a very good fighter. I've had only three fights so far and I didn't do well. Two of them didn't fight fair and naturally got the best of me. The third was with one of my own kind and we ended up being good friends. I guess it was a tie! I'd never brag about my ability to fight and win."

"I could learn ya' to fight good. I've had lots and none of 'em was fair. When they don't fight fair there's no way ya' could win!" The boy was hot on the topic. I guess everyone needs something to brag about even if they don't say it out loud. He softened as he turned to Sal, "My name is Otis Jeffers. What's yours and where ya' headin'?"

"My name is Newt, but one of the boys at school started teasing me - Newt- you know? So I go by Sal! The joke's on me I guess!" and Sal grinned.

Otis looked baffled, "Sal?"

"Yes, a newt is a kind of a Salamander, you know? They live around and under stones in and around a creek. So the name Sal stuck. I'm so glad they didn't call me the whole word. Hard to go through life being called Salamander!" Sal laughed. Otis stared awhile and then chuckled too. Sal knew it wasn't smart to take up with his kind but, darn it! He already liked Otis!

The boys hadn't noticed Otis' father coming back down the path to the gate. It was hard to tell if he'd been hired or not. But, then it was always hard to read his kind. He seemed docile, not ready for a quarrel; rather always ready to avoid one. He was of big build which probably, allowed for others to give him wide berth.

"Come on, boy. She hired me. She's okay for you working with me, but no extra wages. It's going to be hard work for us. We're used to that," he shrugged. "If she likes my work, we'll see." He removed his old straw hat, full of holes, and wiped his brow as though what he'd said was a long speech for him, leaving him breathing hard. "You'd better git along, boy," he waved his hat towards Sal to swoosh him back to the road.

Hearing Serin Jeffers had been hired gave Sal confidence that he might be allowed to sleep the night in the barn; get a fresh start at sun-up. "What is the widow's name Mr. Jeffers?" Sal inquired.

Jeffers turned, looked Sal up and down. "You ain't foolin' me, boy. Your kind ain't so uppity you know, calling me Mr. Jeffers. It won't git ya' nowhere with me. Ask me proper like."

Sal shrugged, looking puzzled. "I just want to sleep in the barn, just for the night. I want to ask the Missus if I can."

"No need. The barn will be ruled by me!" And he poked his thumb to his chest for emphasis. "No, ya' can't stay. Git on with ya'."

Otis turned on his father, "Leave 'im stay Pap. It's gittin' on to dark."

"Please?" Sal pleaded.

Serin lowered his head, took the longest time to respond. Finally, "Okay! But you stay outta' my way and be outta' here by sun-up!" The three turned and headed up the path together. Sal slowed down, leaving some distance between the two up ahead and himself. But he still heard Serin Jeffers reprimand his son, "You know it ain't good for me and you to mix with him and his kind."

Sal woke up and stretched over the hay to get the kinks out. He'd slept well, not noticing or hearing the mice who'd shared the hay pile with him. The sun was already up. He'd better hurry or he might get his hide tanned by the "ruler" of the barn. He tied his few things in the square cloth he had brought with him. He did not have many treasures, except the letter; he'd already checked to make sure it was still in his tunic pocket; the tunic being a looser and cooler garment than most boys wore. He hurried out the back of the barn. As he rounded the corner, he found himself in a pretty little garden. Flowers perfumed the air and showed off colors so beautiful Sal doubted any artist could recreate them. He saw a lady dressed in soft and very expensive looking finery, presenting a lady in every sense of the word, reading from a Bible. She looked up and smiled at Sal, not startled at all.

"Have you been left behind?"

Sal was reticent to become engaged in conversation with her. She might not like the idea of his sleeping on her property. But he couldn't not answer her. Truth always, his father had taught him. "No, Mam, I was not left behind. I slept in the barn last night." He didn't want to implicate Mr. Jeffers so he'd allow her to believe he had trespassed. "And Mr. Jeffers didn't know. I met him at the gate. He didn't know----"

Unexpectedly Serin Jeffers appeared, "What didn't I know?" He stopped to stand next to Sal, which made Sal nervous.

"That this boy stayed the night in the barn." she answered.

Jeffers looked over his shoulder to see his son tripping out of the barn. When Otis realized the widder was present, he stopped short and braced to an attention stance.

Jeffers swallowed hard and spoke to the widow, "I'm sorry Mrs. Fontaine, Mam, he's leaving right now. Needed a place to sleep, just for last night, Mam. Sorry. Mam, I should have asked you. You're the Boss Lady now, Mam. He's on his way down the road. Git along, boy."

Sal looked up at Serin with a different expression on his face. Serin hadn't lied which he could have done. He could have derided Sal and allowed Sal to take the whole blame. But he hadn't and he went up a notch to Sal's way of thinking. He'd have to remember people that were not his kind had their own principles. "I know, Father. Don't judge a man by his cover," Sal almost said aloud. Maybe Otis' father was doing the best he could for his son. Just like Sal's people, life was hard, Sal concluded.

Mrs. Fontaine interrupted, "Allow me to speak with the boy. No harm done, Mr. Jeffers. Get on with the day's work. I'll take care of this lad. Over lunch we'll discuss the farm."

"Yes, Mam, Missus." Serin Jeffers backed away in a subservient manner. "Lunch." And he turned and hurried back to the garden.

When they were gone the widow turned again to Sal, "Come sit by me. Tell me your name and why you are sleeping in barns."

Sal was frightened. He thought for sure he was in trouble; that Mrs. Fontaine didn't want some stray, obviously poor, trespassing on her land. He couldn't fault her; there was so much trouble and hatred in their world during these days.

"My name is Sal Brickers. I'm heading to Baton Rouge. I couldn't find anyone who wanted to take me so I'm walking. I was so tired last night. I'm sorry, Mam. I convinced Mr. Jeffers to let me stay the night in the barn. I should have asked you, Mam."

"I am concerned about you - a boy traveling alone on these back roads. Now where did you say you were going, Sal?" Rather than answer he pulled his father's letter out of his pocket and handed it to her. He watched her closely and saw that she read it twice. Finally she looked up, smiled and asked, "May I have this?"

"No, Mam," he answered quickly. He would not let his father's letter out of his possession.

"Alright," she smiled, "if I give you some paper and quill will you copy it for me? I know Mr. Fayette. I want to write him and see if he will help you further. Is that alright with you?" Not waiting for his answer, she sat quietly in thought. Finally she said, "Since today is Friday, we can't have you to Baton Rouge this week. It' s too far to make it in time. In the meantime you will stay here until I hear from him. Do you agree?

He did, reluctantly. She opened her Bible and apparently the conversation was over. Sal had so hoped that he would see his father within a few days. Oh, well; it was a whole week before Mr. Fayette would be in Baton Rouge again. At least he would have a place to stay even if it was a barn. He sat and used the garden steps as a table. He finished copying the letter, folded it and put the quill back in the ink well.

Mrs. Fontaine closed her Bible and reached for the copied letter in his hand. She read it again. She noticed that Sal hadn't copied it verbatim. The copy was written in a very intelligent hand.

"Sal, I see that you have corrected your father's letter. Not many men have had the opportunity to learn to read and write. I know my husband didn't learn until we were married. It was then that he learned to read, cipher and write some. But he never learned about books, the arts or penning his thoughts in an artful way. But I have a feeling that you have wonderful things to say; things that people should hear and think about." She studied him as though she expected a response from him.

"There is so much I want to learn. My father creates poetry and he has beautiful thoughts and mindful thoughts. People should know the things he knows. I think they call it philosophy, or maybe not. But, anyways he can't write so I write them down to bring them to life. I wish the whole world could know his thoughts. There are lots of people who hate him for no good reason, except to feel superior to him. To me it makes no sense. It wouldn't matter what he thinks if no one listens. My father hates no man regardless of who he is. If he never plowed another field or never gathered another harvest, someone else can pick up and do them. But his thoughts have to be heard. Written down they can live forever. All it takes is for me to write them all down. I have to; the world needs to know how he thinks. Maybe then men will embrace his thoughts and stop hating something like another man's skin color. Someone has to say it. My father will say it and I will write it."

The widow stood quietly observing him as he spoke. Her smile showered him with admiration. Finally she said, "I think you have beautiful thoughts like him. And, you know what? You and your father can write them down for others to read and think about. You are a very fortunate boy. I'll see you at lunch. Until then you might be helping, if Mr. Jeffers needs it. It doesn't hurt for any boy to do some manual work. I'll write to Mr. Fayette this afternoon." She smiled and stepped softly into her home. Sal had never been in the presence of anyone who made him want to play the violin, invent something that would change the world, compose a symphony, or paint the firmament that lifted you up just looking at it. Not even Miss Jennings.

He went to the house garden where he figured Otis and Mr. Jeffers would be. Mr. Jeffers looked at him, "You still here? Thought ya'd be gone by now."

"Mrs. Fontaine will help me to get to my father faster, he explained.

"She's a nice lady."

"Now ya' don't go usin' her jist to help yourself, boy."

Sal was brought down from his elevated reverie with a thud. He'd never do that but he decided to keep quiet about it. "Can I help with something Mr. Jeffers?"

"Well, I'm just kinda' studyin' everything a bit. I need to know what's planted and comin' up, what didn't make it and figure out why. And I need to think about what should be planted to make sure this family is eatin' proper- like. 'Course I'll need to mix som' im' to tickle them seeds into growin'."

The boy looked at him and thought, "Mr. Jeffers might be rough and tumble and sometimes downright ornery, but he knew his work and had the Fontaines' best interest at heart, making sure they ate well and had good nutrition. Of course Mr. Jeffers' kind knew the science of farming; the long hours, the hard work and little or no credit. Well, maybe not all of his kind. Mr. Jeffers had the cruelest life, but then so did Sal's father. They did it all so other people could eat and get rich. If Mr. Jeffers could read and write, he could put down on paper what he knew so those that didn't know how would be able to farm just by following his advice. And Cab, his father, could offer people the opportunity to think loftier thoughts and live by the goodness expressed by his father. His words created peace. Everyone can learn and keep on learning.

"A bit of advice, boy. Don't mess up!" was Mr. Jeffers advice right now.

Sal felt sorry for him. But he also knew that Mr. Jeffers felt sorry for Cab Brickers, Sal's father.

"Boy, ya' kin count the rows devoted to potatoes, squash, cabbage,--all the vegetables. Kin ya' cipher?"

"Yes, I can. And Mr. Jeffers, my name is Sal."

"Okay, boy. Git to it." Sal sighed and started counting.

Otis had over-heard the interchange between his pap and Sal. He shook his head and grinned.

Otis was getting his hands dirty. He saw no dirt in ciphering. And that was a sight to see. Days passed. Otis still got dirty and Sal still wrote for Pap and ciphered long lists for Pap. The plowing turned over rich soil that any farmer would crave. (Pap had given Sal permission to call him by his first name and as Pap got to see and appreciate Sal's skills and willingness for dirty work as well, he promised to try and call Sal by his first name.

Serin often gave both boys accolades for 'running the race well'. He'd storied them about meeting a man some years ago who was sitting on a stump of a tree, reading the Bible. In the middle of the day, no less. Folks usually read the Bible in the morning or at night by the fireside. "I set down near him on one of many stumps; must be some landowner had sold his trees for lumber. 'Enaways the reader and I took up talkin' to each other. He could tell I was bummed and down. I told 'im I worked and worked and didn't git nowhere. He told me there was this guy, Paul, in the Bible. He took up with these 'early Christians, whatever. 'Enaways this Paul talked about when the Lord (I was pretty sure Paul was really big on the Lord)-um-meets us at the Pearly Gates- I think he meant Heaven-whatever-when ya' meet 'im the Lord will say to those who did work hard all their lifes-he'd say to them 'Race well run.' Go over there at them there gates and enter Heaven. "So boys, I'm sayin' race well run! I can't gitcha' in the Pearly Gates; but your work these past few days makes me wisht' I had Pearly sumim' for ya's both. So, boys, race well run. That guy on the stump told me to "always keep your eyes on the prize." Now I ain't so smart but I think the prize is Heaven. Yep! I always say when I can't get the dirt out from under my finger nails; here I come Lord! I worked the life of five men and still claim a race well run. "And he smiled, looked heavenward and yelled, "I' m coming for my prize, Lord!"

Sal was liking Serin more and more every day. He was a good man. But he still continued to instill fear in Sal when things were not going well. His compliments were few and far between. It was good for the boy to take pride in manual labor as well as scholarly endeavors.

Mr. Fayette was contacted and answered Mrs. Fontaine's letter. He would pick Sal up here at the plantation. He accepted her invitation to stay a day or two before heading back to New Orleans. However he could not do it the following week but the next week would be fine. He would arrive on Thursday and spend the day visiting and assessing the plight of the Fontaines' situation for ways he could help them at this grieving time. Friday he had work in Baton Rouge. He would return to the plantation that night and leave early Saturday morning with Sal as his traveling companion.

Sal was disappointed to delay another week but he had no choice. Walking to Baton Rouge was a daunting task; but to New Orleans, almost impossible. He'd just have to wait.

He was happy working with Otis and Serin. It made him feel like a man. No wonder Otis had so much spunk; he did the work of a man. And he was fun to be around. Another plus was Mrs. Fontaine had asked Sal to spend an hour each evening reading to her children. The Fontaine library was a treasure! He was granted the privilege of choosing a book to his liking! He was in Heaven! He chose a new adventure book, "The Shipwrecked Irish Boy." Reading was not work and somehow he was certain Mrs. Fontaine had him in mind as well as her children.

Otis, as hard as he worked, had new-found energy in the evening. He was jolly and fun-loving and ready for anything. He was also a master schemer. One night he called Sal to the barn. Sal entered and was barraged with horse balls. Sal lowered his head to prevent eating one and dived into Otis, knocking him off-balance. Otis fell to the floor with his opponent still grasping his arms tightly so he was unable to get Sal off him. Soon Sal was rubbing horse balls into Otis' thick mane of hair. "ew, ew!" was Otis' come back. Sal arose carefully so he couldn't be captured himself.

Otis got up, lowered his head, using his hands to brush excrement from his hair. Sal stayed a safe distance in case Otis had another idea. But, no, he started laughing and said, "I thought you couldn't fight? You are a hustler!"

"No, I'm not. It was a stinking thing to do Otis. Watch your back, boy."

Otis put up his dukes and said, "Don't call me boy, boy."

"Now this is where I walk off the stage."

He laughed and Otis laughed. "We better head to the pond 'afore Pap declares to use us for fertilizer." They threw their arms around each others' shoulders and headed for a bath.

Pranks looked for Otis, but a few nights later both boys met up with trouble. After supper Otis spread out under a huge elm tree. No denying it was cooler there. Sal had finished his reading task. He saw Otis and lay down beside him to cool off.

"Hey, Otis,"

"Hey, Salamander."

Sal poked Otis' ribs with an elbow punch. "Funny. Very funny."

"I thought so," was the come-back. "Whatcha' wanta' do?"

"I don't know, but at the moment I'm thirsty."

Otis rolled over, facing Sal. "How 'bout I git us som'em to drink and I'll meet you down at the pond?"

"Okay." Sal turned over and sat up. He looked Otis in the eye, "Nice cool water."

"Yeh. Yeh."

Sal was waiting on the bank. He looked over his shoulder and saw Otis coming with a burlap sack slung over his shoulder. "Man, I'm thirsty." Otis put his hand inside the sack and pulled out a bottle. "Here, drink like a man."

"What is it?" and he grabbed the bottle, pulled out the plug and took a whiff.

"Phew, what is this? It smells like whiskey!"

"That's 'cause it's whiskey," and Otis laughed.

"Where'd you get this, Otis?"

"Don't matter none where I got it. Take a swig!"

Sal raised the bottle to his mouth, swallowed and started coughing. It burned all the way to his stomach. "Good Lord, that stings!" Otis laughed again and took a big swig. He tried not to cough so Sal would think Otis was more growed up than he was.

To tell the truth Sal did admire Otis' confidence. "But what I want to know is where this came from. I mean it, Otis."

"Aw right, aw right!" I snuck it from the house." He smiled. He was proud of his caper.

"Aw Otis. We're in big trouble now. And Mrs. Fontaine is so good to us!"

"Don't worry. We'll just take a couple of swigs, plug it up again. I got it outta' there- I'll git it back." "I hope so!" Sal didn't want to visualize Otis creeping around inside the manor.

"Here, take a last swig 'afore me and that'll be it." Sal did. His head started to feel funny. Wow! Otis held the bottle up to his mouth, tipped it up and saw Pap rumbling toward him with that black look he got when he was all stirred up in anger. Otis swallowed and looked sheepishly at Pap.

"Ah, boys, pushin' to be big shots? Well, I guess all boys have to grow up sum'time. Now's as good as ever. Sal, take another swig. Your turn. Now Son, take a swig like a man."

Otis threw his shoulders back, his chest out and proudly took a big swig. Sal thought, "Otis isn't getting this at all. He thinks his father was encouraging this charade." Something told Sal that Serin would make them pay for their stupidity and making them drink more was the payoff. Sal took just a sip the next time around.

"That's nuff', Men." Serin said. "Now you men git some sleep. You'll need it tomorrow."

Sal was already regretting. His stomach swirled and he found he had to rush to the outhouse! Otis went right to bed. Maybe he did have more experience.

Next morning the barn roiled with hangover. Sal swore to himself he would never swig a whiskey again. Otis refused to look at Sal and grumbled all morning. Both boys rejected breakfast. Mrs. Fontaine noticed but did not question. She never mentioned the whiskey; maybe it magically reappeared as it had magically disappeared.

The days rolled by slowly for Sal but tomorrow Mr. Fayette would arrive for his visit with Mrs. Fontaine. And Saturday was THE day. Just two more days.

Sal had to admit he enjoyed working in the garden. Even in the soil. Otis watched covertly and was surprised how Sal knew how to do things. Of course he knew Sal's father had been forced to work just as his own pap had even allowing that they were different people. And Otis knew they could not be real friends for much longer. Why was the world the way it was? Maybe Sal's kind knew the answer to that. There was always something in their eyes that gave them the privilege of understanding the prejudice that enveloped ordinary men, one against the other. Knowing didn't stop them from prejudice nor did imagined superiority. Otis hated to see Sal go. They had been friends. Maybe if all different people could work and laugh together and live together as a big family, like he and Sal, just the two of them, had done, the world could be a better place. Men needn't be afraid to walk lonely roads or to be sold like animals to the slaughter. Otis and Sal agreed to all these 'what ifs.'

And the most important thing was they needed each other. Sal made a record of all Serin did and accomplished. Otis was strong and hardworking doing the labor work. Sometimes he helped Sal do the counting and the record information. And sometimes Sal surprised them by getting dirty, too.

Finally it was Saturday! and it was still dark, not yet sun-up. Sal climbed into the carriage. Sal looked back from the carriage and smiled. Pap and Otis saluted him. Then Otis started swinging something upside down. Sal squinted and started laughing at the whiskey bottle. And the carriage, headed to New Orleans, disappeared around the bend.

Otis knocked softly on the manor door and Mrs. Fontaine unlatched it and said, "Come in Otis. You have a serious look on your face. Are you troubled, or your father?"

"No, Mam, Boss Lady, I was kinda' hoping you would read this letter for me."

She took the letter and opened it, looked back at Otis and she began reading:

> Otis, my friend, I will never forget you. Maybe
> you will come to New Orleans someday and visit
> me. I want you to know that I admire you and

your Pap. You are good people under that rugged attitude. Your kindness helped Mrs. Fontaine and her family. I will never forget how you patted my back when I told you I would not see my father for two more weeks. You must have stayed awake at night thinking up all those things to make my days go faster. Thank you. You are a good friend.

And Serin, no I mean Mr. Jeffers (you deserve to be addressed that way,) I will see you in Heaven. You run a good race, just like that guy Paul said. You taught me to run one too. I'll never forget to keep running the good race and keeping my eye on the prize, thanks to you.

To both of you, thank you for be-friending a lonely colored boy---who ended up having incredible white friends.

Your friend, Sal (Newt Brickers)

THE LEAST
OF THESE

A Short Story
By
Mary Jane Casey Lane

He knew the doors to St. Vincent's Church would not be unlocked at 1:15 am. He'd hoped but was disappointed to find them locked. He reminded himself that he still did foolish things even though he'd mostly been wrong in the past. I guess you can't teach new tricks to old fogies like himself. "Okay," he thought, "maybe a window would be open." He circled the church and it didn't look promising - all stain glass with small openings; he couldn't enter through any of those. He circled again; maybe he'd missed something. There were no lights in the rectory. As long as he was quiet he didn't think detection was likely. Sure enough he saw a window in the back that cowered in a humble clear glass pane surrounded by artistic and beautiful depictions in glass in every other window making up the church. Surely it felt like a misfit. It made him think of a window for a kitchen. Not a promising idea to actually enter via a lived-in room. But then again, kitchen or not, it was highly unlikely that clergy or staff (housekeeper, or cook) would reside in the church itself. You'd never see a kitchen in the church proper. Okay, so it was probably a window in the sacristy or even a hallway "Well one way to find out, old man. Try the lock on the window and hope it will open quietly. I could say a prayer that it would open. Nah, not a good idea, asking the Lord to aid and abet!"

He dragged a trash can to the window and, with a grunt, climbed up and peered in. Yep, it was the sacristy. The light from the full moon was just right. He could make out a table on which there were placed cruets, a glass tray and a basket of altar linens. He'd been an altar boy and recognized them even though it was dark. He knew their shapes and identified them. Now for the lock. Wonder of wonders, the window was unlocked! Father Rakoczy should know his maintenance man hadn't locked this easily accessible window. No security alarm. Another stroke of good luck. Soon he found himself standing in the sacristy, and with his flash light, checking the candlesticks he'd held carefully under his jacket in transportation from his cart to the sacristy. No dents or scratches! Soon he was back in the sacristy, having placed the candlesticks on the main altar. He hoped he'd guessed correctly the place from which they were taken. Out the window, around the church and finally on the sidewalk in front, where he had left his shopping cart holding all his earthly possessions. He strolled down Church Street. As soon as he saw the expressway bridge, he stepped it up. He was tired. It had been a long day. The bridge abutment was bordered by bushes in full bloom. In another season their branches would be naked and thus unable to hide his make-shift bedroom. He wouldn't need his tarp tonight - no rain expected. Just lie down, cover with some trash bags and drop off to sleep. The constant hum of traffic on the highway overhead helped to lull him off to sleep. And he slipped softly into the fantasy of dreams and contentment. All was good in his life.

****

The late spring sun rise woke him to a warm breeze and the promise of a comfortable day. He stretched and slowly opened his eyes and smiled. He feasted his eyes on the pretty pink blossoms adorning the bush next to his bed. He wouldn't know exactly what time it was until he began his work day, strolling back to the church. The bell tower was faced with a large ornate clock. Either the bells would toll out the hour for him or, as he moved nearer, he could see the exact time. Like all homeless he'd lost all his valuable possessions, either stolen from him during the night and sold for whatever sustenance they relied on, usually booze, or his pocket had been picked. In Moses' case he had no idea what had become of his wristwatch. Before starting to work he'd head to the homeless shelter for oatmeal; he'd missed supper last night. Most of yesterday had been taken up with the candlesticks' discovery and a blueprint for their return. Not an easy day. Negotiations had spent entirely too much time. He'd have to touch base again with the young lad sometime today. After breakfast he washed up and brushed his teeth, one luxury he allowed himself, at the bus depot downtown at Main and Delaware. His tube of tooth paste was nearing empty. He had to remember to tell Alice, the Director of the Shelter, to get him some. It was 9 am. Late for the start of his day but his fellow homeless companions had tied him up in a political debate, over breakfast. Which had he been honest he had no idea what he thought. But friends were friends and friendship had to be nurtured.

Main Street was busier than usual. Maybe it was Saturday. Living his life seldom required knowing the day of the week. He came to the corner with his cart and waited to cross Delaware. A small girl ran up to the corner, though he could hear the father behind shouting for her to stop. She had momentum pushing her into the street as cars zoomed by; she ran into the lane of a speeding van. Moses left his cart and rushed into the street and threw her back to the curb. She had a few scrapes but otherwise she was okay. In her fright she was screaming and sobbing as her father rushed to her. Moses' body was side-swiped and landed near the curb but still in the street. He heard police whistles, many voices asking if he was alright. Some walked right on by, not interested in his plight. Maybe they had shopping to do or another priority--whatever. He didn't know whether he was alright or not, the shock still pummeling his body. A cop appeared and told him not to move because an ambulance was on its way. "Dear Lord," he thought, "I don't need paramedics!" He tried to tell the officer he wasn't hurt, but to no avail. He heard the siren of the ambulance and next thing he knew he was being placed on a gurney. "My cart! My cart! I need it. It has all my possessions in it!"

"We'll take it to the precinct and you can pick it up when you are released from the hospital. You seem to be alright but better to play it safe. I promise, old man, I'll take the cart with me. Good luck, now." Fortunately Moses had no injuries; but at the doctor's advice he spent the night. But the doctor taking care of him in the ER warned him he'd probably be bruised and sore. "However, I'm not comfortable without an address for you. And the authorities will probably be in to question you further," the doctor informed him.

"My address would be the Shelter on Canal Street," Moses lied. Not really a lie because if he weren't on this assignment his address would be the shelter. If the powers that be got too snoopy, it would interfere with his work. But, of course he couldn't tell them that. He tried to calm himself by breathing in, holding the breath and then exhaling slowly. It usually worked for him. Better to relax while he could, before they sent him on his way.

"Moses Shandley?" A policeman and another man were standing just inside his room. So much for relaxing. The man next to the police man was holding his hat in front of him and he was turning the brim around and around in his hands. Moses thought the man was nervous about something but it turned out to be a habit. He certainly wasn't nervous, Moses realized when the man spoke up. Moses nodded and they moved toward him.

The policeman explained, "This is Mr. Nobles. You saved his daughter from being hit by that van. He'd like to talk to you."

Oh, no! "How is your little girl, Mr. Nobles?"

"She was frightened but no injuries. I' m told you were spared injuries too. That's good news! Mr. Shandley, how can we thank you? It was a very brave thing you did. And we want to thank you somehow. I think you are a homeless man. How can we help. We' re offering a reward, and----"

Moses jumped in quickly, "No, no; no reward! I need nothing. But thank you for offering," he stammered.

"Mr. Shandley, do you have children?"

"I did once." Careful, old man. Take this in another direction. "And I know that your daughter means the world to you. Officer, could I speak privately with Mr. Nobles?"

"Of course." And more to Nobles than Moses, "I'll be right outside the door."

"Mr. Nobles, I'm going to tell you something I never discuss with anyone. You are a husband and a father. You'd do anything for them; any sacrifice- right?" Nobles nodded yes. "Well, I can't explain but I need to live this life style. So, when I say that your appreciation would change what my world must be, I think you can understand. I am so thankful I was there to help your little girl, but please allow me my privacy. Father to Father; man to man. Please?"

"I don't really understand Mr. Shandley; but then I don't need to if it is what you want. Know that, in our eyes, you are a hero. Would you allow us that?" Noble pleaded. He continued to twirl his hat.

"I would. I would. I believe you are a noble man, no pun intended," and he smiled weakly. "And thank you."

"We are the ones who are thankful. Is it alright if we pray for you?"

"You bet! I need it." Moses answered.

"Don't we all!" And Mr. Nobles turned and left Moses to himself. The doctor returned and discharged Moses. He was so relieved. No fuss. No fanfare. He felt secure again.

He walked to the ninth precinct. The officer who had helped in the caper yesterday was not on duty today. That really worried Moses. He needed his cart. He couldn't remember all that was among his possessions; he only hoped that there wasn't anything to cause suspicion or give him away. Another officer spoke to him, and checked on the grocery cart. Moses was relieved to see him pushing the cart toward him. "What is your address?" the police man asked.

"I stay at the shelter. On Canal Street," he lied again.

The officer looked doubtful. "Well we could arrest you for vagrancy, you know."

"Oh, no, God, please help me." Moses' troubled mind pleaded. "Actually I'm looking for a job, Officer," he was really stacking up so many untruths, it made him nervous, "Please give me more time to clean up my life?" Now that was the truth he told himself. The officer thought a minute. Moses knew he was chewing his lower lip, which he did when he was nervous. "You'd better go out the back entrance. Fewer people to encounter. But Moses, know that I will be keeping tabs on you."

"Right." And thank you Officer um-----"

"McAllen. Get out of here before I change my mind."

Moses was already down the hall looking for the back exit.

Officer McAllen shook his head. A strange man, this Moses! He doesn't sound like a homeless but no verifiable address. And I let him get away without asking how he was able to take possession of a grocery cart.

****

Moses stopped at a bench and reorganized his belongings, which the police had obviously searched through. He walked to the West Side to the corner of Park Avenue and Madison Street, the corner where young girls flaunted their assets for anyone interested. Two caught his attention immediately. They were heavily made-up, one a red head. A sprayed on redhead not a naturally born one. Clown head! The two standing in front of the store front approached two others, who appeared to be new-comers at the curb. "Get lost, Sleeping Beauties. This is our corner," one of them sneered. "Move your asses down to Maple," which was a couple of blocks and not a lucrative corner for them. Any john would have already picked up a girl by the time he approached Maple.

Moses walked casually pushing his cart. He stopped at the store front and smiled at the 'owners' of that corner.

"Mister Homeless Guy, you can't afford us so move along. And we already have a pimp; so shop someplace else."

He did not move. "Do you girls know what you are doing to yourselves?

The dangers of this business? Violence, HIV or STD?"

One of the girls, the one with the bigger attitude, sneered, "Oh, look here! A tramp who thinks he's a preacher! Back off Reverend."

"If you want out of the business I can help you."

"Okay. Give me a thousand dollars and I'll join the convent," And she held out her hand. He shook his head; marveling at their lack of self-esteem.

"Just let m---," and a car pulled up to the curb. The driver lowered the passenger side window.

"Is this man bothering you girls?"

"Yes, he scares us!" declared the more theatrical one.

The driver told Moses to back-off. "Get in girls-yes, both of you —this man is dangerous. He might hurt you. Come on, don't take any chances."

The girls hopped in the car not knowing they were taking even bigger chances and were in more danger now. More than Moses wanted to think about.

He headed down to speak to the two who had just been deported from Madison and Park Avenue. Half way down to Maple one of the two was approached and had accepted the deal. As the car pulled away, the one left alone turned toward the building at the corner and Moses could see that she was sobbing. He stepped it up to help her. "Come on now, Honey. You're still safe but I'm afraid your friend's not."

She tried to quickly brush away the tears. She looked at him and trembled even more. She gulped, "What are ya' looking for? I' m sure I can do anything you w-w-want." And she began to cry again. A pause. "I'm sorry. I can't go with you. I just can't!"

"You need money?"

"Y-y-yes. But I can't get it this way. I'm sorry!"

Moses knew enough not to touch her; so he quietly asked, "See that bench further down Madison? Let' s go sit and see what we can do about your situation. We'll be in plain view of the hundreds of cars passing by. You'll be perfectly safe; and I promise you, even if I am a homeless, I can help you outta' this situation. Walk ahead of me to the bench. Okay?" She turned and walked further down the street, very frightened, checking her surroundings.

As Moses settled down next to the girl, she moved as far away from him as she could on the bench. He stated, "There are several ways we can go with this. What do you think you want to do? I don't really know your story. What is your name?"

"Trudy," and she began to sob uncontrollably. "I just want to go home. I want my mama. But I don't have any money so I can't go home until I make some!"

"No more thoughts of 'making' it. You can't live on the streets to make money. Where do you hail from?"

"Toledo, Ohio. I want to go home!" and she began to sob again.

"Okay, okay." He tried to comfort her. "The fact that you want to go home, that makes it easier." In her shock at hearing this she snapped to attention, "It is? But bus tickets cost money and I don't have any." She didn't break down this time, sensing that she was beginning to believe Moses could help her even if he was a homeless guy. And she needn't fear him. But surely he didn't have any money. She searched his face for the answer.

"We have to see how much for a bus ticket to home," he stated.

She thought a minute. "It cost me $130 dollars when I came here. Where will you get that kind of money?" she asked.

"Just wait here. I'll find a telephone booth and come back with the information we need to get you outta' this mess. You know the decision to go back home shows that you are really a good person. Think of that when the questions at home tend to discourage you. Say it over and over, "I'm really a good person."

She brightened, "Wait, I have a cell phone still charged. I checked it; still working. Here. You'll give it back, right?"

From Moses' point of view, that question didn't deserve an answer. Moses took the phone, dialed and waited, "This is Moses. I need $150 dollars to send a potential street girl home. Yes. Yes. This is for sure!" He began to look frustrated, "I'll purchase the ticket myself. Okay," and he turned toward the girl, "we have to be careful, Trudy, some girls would say yes and then just use the money and not go home—Yeah? Okay I'll bring her over for the night unless she can grab a bus today. If tomorrow then we'll see ya' later. Yeah, (pause) yeah. I'll wait for him to get the money to me. And, Frank, thanks, brother. Now tell Sam to hustle down here."

"Trudy, I'll walk to the bus depot and check things out. There's a McDonald's at the corner of Main and this street, Madison. I'll turn right at Main but you wait for me there. Here's two dollars, all I got right now. Eat something or at least a drink. You walk ahead of me. You shouldn't be seen as too familiar with me. I'll be in back pacing myself to stay behind. Say a prayer of thanks; your troubles are over. I'll see to that. And please wash off that make-up. It's a dead giveaway." Trudy looked at her reflection in a store-front window. "Oh, my God!"

As it worked out Trudy had boarded a bus to home at 4 pm.

Moses stayed near-by until she was safely on the bus. Her face was still red from her scrubbing earlier. "I didn't think she'd ever stop crying," he thought.

****

Moses was hungry and went back to the shelter. Meatloaf tonight. He didn't know where in the community lived the person who made it. But it was worth more walking to sit at that meal! He looked forward to his bedroom. It was a beautiful evening. He'd stop at the railroad bridge where his friend, Hobo, slept in a card board bedroom, as Moses did in the cold weather. Hopefully Hobo had a poker game scheduled. He hadn't forgotten to check for his cigar box when reorganizing his cart after picking it up at the precinct. He was in good shape; he had over 200 used matches, more than enough to get into the game. He'd had a fruitful day, getting Trudy home where she should be---great day!

Someone was rifling among his things in the cart! He didn't open his eyes yet. Slowly he turned as though tumbling in his sleep. More digging sounds. He opened one eye, then both, "Puddle, what the hell are you doing? What are ya' looking for?" Puddle, simple minded, gained his nickname because his shoes were always wet. Don't know where he went for that to happen; maybe, as some of the guys thought, urine was the explanation. The smell of Puddle kind of confirmed it.

****

"Sorry, Moses, I'm just so hungry. I hoped I'd find something in your cart, a cookie or an apple core, ya' know?"

That sent Moses' heart to that place where he almost despaired. "But, no. Don't go to despair, even for Puddle!" he thought, "One step at a time."

"Aw, Puddle I don't have anything-wait! I think I do have a dentine!" He got up and rummaged through his things and found the gum in a pocket inside his jacket, the one with a zipper. "They tell people on a diet to chew gum when they are hungry so they won't eat something they shouldn't. It takes the hunger away. Here."

"Thanks Moses, 'cept I ain't on a diet."

Moses chuckled, "Keep chewing, you'll see. Now go lie down and go to sleep. In the morning I'll take you to the shelter for oatmeal. M-m, good. Night Puddle." He heard Puddle arranging his newspaper blankets over himself. Moses wished he could find a way to take care of him. He was like a child and that worried Moses. Life could interrupt Puddle's existence in frightful ways. They were looking for sources that would help Puddle. It was slow-going.

****

The homeless never gave out their real names; so they each adopted a "Homeless Name". Moses chose Moses for no particular reason. Most times your name was selected by the people in your circle of life. And it usually came from a physical characteristic or a habit you exhibited or an activity that kept you a suspect to others. There were the obvious ones: Meathead, Moe, Pops, The Prick (excuse me), Too Tall, Nick the Knife (they tried to avoid him as much as possible; there were a couple men who'd antagonized him and had scars to prove it), Rocky, Boo, Fish Head, The Rat etc. etc. We had one gay homeless called Bo Peep. 'Moses' was pretty acceptable by comparison. There were few women homeless on this side of town. They tended to settle in and around the East End.

****

Moses skipped the morning ritual toilette because of Puddle. There were some things the other homeless did not need to know. They reached the shelter, had their oatmeal (other foods were offered but Moses always took the oatmeal.) Puddle eyed the pastries but because Moses didn't take them, neither did he.

"Do you have your day planned, Puddle?" And Moses flipped an apple into Puddle's jacket.

"Oh, yeah, several personal things to tend to. You know what I mean?"

"Yeah, I do, Puddle." Puddle didn't have anything planned for the day. But there were some things all homeless had to honor- dignity in others' choices and privacy were the top two. So Moses dropped the conversation. "Okay, then I'll be on my way. I have some business to take care of too. See ya' around."

Puddle nodded and didn't believe Moses either. Such was the world of the Homeless.

****

Moses thought to himself, "I need to find the lad. He was so close! And I fear for his addiction. At least he didn't have the candlesticks to fence with the temptation to buy."

Moses headed to the vacant and abandoned tenements a mile, or more likely two, down Canal Street. He had more stamina and could walk further than when he'd first turned to this way of life. Minimal diet and more exercise. He'd probably live to be a hundred! "Look out, Richard Simmons, Moses is in the house!" Not exactly an Atkins model for losing weight, but, hey, it works! Moses was living proof. A 3-Step Program: Step 1: Steal a cart. Step 2: Run to your local dumpster and plan your meals. Step 3: Walk everywhere, all day (Not at least 3x a week, or at least 30 minutes a day but all day, every day.) If you don't lose weight, we'll gladly refund your empty beer cans. Guaranteed! "I'm a hit! And truthfully no competition. You'd better try comedy, Ole Boy!"

Finally he came to the tenement he was looking for. He walked all the way around the complex and did not see the boy, whose name Moses didn't know. He had to rest: he sat on the steps to one of the run-down entrances. He'd worked up a sweat. As he reached for a dirty towel from his cart to dry his forehead, he heard, "Hey, Moses," and a young boy ran from his friends to where Moses was sitting. "Remember me? I'm Ben. You tried to talk me outta' selling drugs last summer?"

"Oh, yes. Did it work?"

"Nope." Wonder of wonders!

"Why not?" Moses challenged.

"Man, I'm making moolah!" and signaling his success by rubbing his thumb against his first two fingers. I'm probably the richest kid in the jungle," and he swept his hand out to include all of the tenement, clearly a falsehood. Boasting. He hadn't been in the business long enough to own this territory.

"And what about your habit, Ben?"

"I don't got a habit no more. Maybe just on holidays. Ya' know what I mean? Somethin' special."

"Yeah, I know what you mean. You still have the habit!"

"Aw come on now, ya' oughta' congratulate me, Mos-ass!" and he purposely mispronounced Moses' name.

"Yeah, maybe I should, because the next time I see you, you'll be sleeping in Haney's Funeral Home with a "Do not Disturb" sign on your casket; too late for congratulations."

"Not me, Moses, I got my strength right here, and he pointed to his two body guards, maybe seventeen years old but stocky and strong looking, supposed to scare more than violent. Ben nodded to the street and they all walked away.

Moses shouted out, "There all kinds of ways to die, Ben."

Ben didn't look back but spread his arms out and shrugged, like he had no fears.

Enough resting, move on. Encounters like this always upset Moses; racked up as a loss. As he rolled back to the street he saw a group of boys playing basketball. He approached the group, "Any of you boys know where I can buy?"

"Oh, no mister, They ain't no sellers around here. It's against the law." And the group all laughed. Moses put a wide grin on his face. "Yeah, but me and my guys down at the rail road bridge could buy elsewhere." The boys looked from one to another, several nodded. They did not want to be found guilty of directing a buyer to another seller. There was a code in the tenements. Dead meat if they were found out. "Okay, mister. Fifth building down that way. It looks

Mary Jane Casey Lane

like no one's there, but there is. Watch yourself though. Those guys don't fool around."

"Thanks," and Moses turned in the direction pointed out to him. He got as far as the entrance and a human strong-hold stopped him from entering.

"Coonie, ya' got a visitor," the mammoth doorman shouted.

"Buyin' or sell in?"

"Doin' a canvas." Moses shouted so Coonie could hear.

"Got a badge or search warrant Canvas Man?"

"No. I want some info about one of your buyers."

"No can do."

"If I buy?"

"Nope."

"Damn, you're a hard nut to deal with." And he grinned at the muscled doorkeeper.

"Let him in, Bonkers." Bonkers frisked Moses, looking for weapons.

"Is my cart safe out here, Bonkers."

"Looks pretty tempting so I'll keep my eyes peeled." was his sarcastic return.

Moses entered trying not to show his nervousness. These kids could be very dangerous. It took a minute for his eyes to adjust to the inner darkness. When they did he saw a kid sitting at a desk. He looked 7 years old, though Moses knew

194

he was not. He reminded Moses of the Beaver on the TV show, LEAVE IT TO BEAVER, a sweet looking face. To himself, "Don't look surprised Moses, Junior probably has a Napoleon complex." He waited for the boy to address him.

"You have 2 minutes to conduct your canvas, starting now," Little Napoleon said.

I'm looking for a boy who was in possession of two very expensive candlesticks. Not a very bright boy though because he hit a policeman's home; a very accomplished man on the squad, decorated for some heroic deed. He has the whole precinct out looking for him. I know he's a customer of yours, big habit and hangs around other Big Habits. They buy from you. If caught, there go your profits behind bars and maybe eager to tell and cop a plea. Thought you should know. Also, I can help the kid disappear where no cop can find him. I owe his family a big favor. So do you know where he is?"

"There was a kid who told Bonkers he had candlesticks from a church. Would we take them as payment for his favorite product. We sell several products - quality only. His choice is very expensive – he mixes- OxyContin and Percocet. He must be high 24 hours a day. I want his business but unfortunately I don't know his street name." Bonkers signaled his boss, "I know his name, if you want it."

"I want it, Bonkers. Good job." Give Bonkers a gold star. A warm fuzzy from the boss!

"They call him Slippery, 'cause he is fast and can disappear right in front of your eyes. If he gets wind that this Canvas guy is looking for him, he'll slip away."

"Do we get paid for this info?" Coonie asked Moses.

"From a homeless victim? Need I answer?"

"So you're not buying today, but I'll see you soon, right?" Moses nodded to the affirmative, "Okay, Homeless Canvas Guy. Slippery is probably hanging around the dock behind the tenements. He watches our product men unload the ship, hoping when he beats it over here his product will have arrived. Look for him at the docks. Go, I'm done with you. Bonkers."

Bonkers grabbed Moses by the arm and literally shoved him out the door. He swung the cart around so the handle was facing Moses, reminding him of the doormen at the Hilton. Except no brass buttons. Probably brass knuckles, his signature. No tip either to a doorman who doesn't show respect. "And I was going to give him a Jackson."

****

As he walked toward the docks the squalor sickened him. Babies, snot-nosed and still in diapers and only a tee shirt, sucking their thumbs, either backed away from Moses or approached his cart and walked along with him. He smiled at them even though they shouldn't trust him and he knew it. A mother called to them in their native tongue; another scurried over to pull her little ones to safety. "Please, God, find a decent life for these future addicts and prostitutes," Moses whispered. "Ah, good the dock is in sight."

A ship was in dock, men unloading so fast it looked like an old silent movie scene. Only a few boys lingered to watch. Moses spotted him. He continued to walk slowly toward them. One boy elbowed another and gestured toward Moses. The other turned slowly and took in Moses and his cart. He recognized Moses. His body language changed to 'alert mode'.

He started to bolt until he realized the dock had only one direction, straight toward Moses.

Moses kept heading toward the dock. He smiled hoping it would somehow engage the kid. Slippery searched for an escape, now in a panic mode. Moses was determined to confront him. Before it registered with him Slippery dived into the water. Standing at the very edge of the dock Moses waited for the boy to re-surface. He couldn't hold his breath forever. Waiting! But he could hold it pretty long. Finally Slippery's hands showed, grabbing the edge of the dock to keep his head above the water. Moses leaned down, "How are ya' doing, Slip?"

"Get lost Ole' Man! Can't ya' see I'm busy?" He wanted to sound tough but Moses saw some apprehension on his face. Either the boy was afraid of him; or respected him. Unlikely the first, hopefully respect because that meant he might actually listen to Moses and allow him to help him deal with the addiction.

"You don't have to live like this. You've got smarts. Let me help you to another safer place. It will take guts, but you've got guts in spades. No police, just re-hab. Whata' ya' say'n and Moses reached down to help the kid back onto the dock. Before they touched skin to skin, Slippery slipped away. Moses walked the whole dock, back and forth, looking for where the boy was coming up for air. He was a slippery little runt! "Come on, boy!" Moses muttered.

Suddenly one of the longshoremen could be heard shouting "What the hell?" He pointed under the dock and through the wooden slats they saw a body visible, but strangely in a vertical position but not paddling. Silence as each man on the dock had a look. Silence!! It was Slippery. Moses dived in and found Slippery caught in some twisted wire attached to the dock uprights, all under water. Moses struggled with the wire. He just couldn't hold his breath that long. He surfaced, "He's caught in wire. I couldn't r----" and one of the longshoremen dived in. All the others (except for one of the kids who was talking to 911) waited for the diver to resurface. Finally he did and shook his head to negative. "Oh, God," Moses prayed. It was not an expletive, a prayer!

The paramedics waited until the coast guard sent a couple of divers. But to no avail. Moses stayed around until the body was finally placed in a body bag. He was questioned. "No" he didn't know his real name; "No" he didn't know where he was living; "No" he didn't know where his parents might be so they could be informed; "No-no-no- no!" He sat down on the dock. He felt so responsible; if he hadn't searched him out. Maybe this life he'd adopted really wasn't helping anyone. "Oh, yes, a girl, was off the streets---one girl! But three others still out there involved in such danger. Addiction, buyers-sellers. Street gangs, teen prostitutes, rape, abuse; violence right outside your front door! To stop it just might be impossible! Why was he doing this? He knew the answer but maybe it didn't work!

The police arrived. The officer who had seen Moses in the hospital a few days ago, "You again?" Moses nodded; he was exhausted. He told his story, concern for the kid. He did not expose any of the tenement kids he'd met. Just that he'd tried to help the kid. He explained that he thought the kid would have listened to him because he was an older f---up and needed to be heard-trying to help the young avoid some of his own mistakes. Speaking to himself, "I was so positive it would work. But now I have my doubts."

"Maybe you were buying?" the officer raised one eyebrow, in an attempt to intimidate Moses.

Moses nodded a simple 'no' and stood up and grabbed his cart, anxious to get out of there. The press was there with flashes one after another. He hurried away.

****

No bedroom tonight. And no supper. He didn't care; he wasn't hungry. When he reached the shelter, Frank was still there in his tiny office with his record books. Moses stood in his doorway, weary and worn. And wet!

Frank closed his laptop and came around his desk and went to the dining room. Moses followed. All in silence. Frank sat at a table and motioned Moses to do the same. He sat down across from Frank and told the whole story, including his anxiety and discouragement. Frank, always a good listener, didn't speak during Moses' soliloquy. Moses ended his story, out of breath. He was finding it difficult to breathe.

Frank gave him a minute and then responded, "It's awful what you experienced today. And I can understand your doubts about what you are doing here. I can't tell you what to do because my part in this does not get me down and dirty like your work does. So as far as advising you what to do, I have to say it's for you to decide; but, Moses, I will challenge you. I insist that you go back to the very beginning and think it through as you did 'way back when'. Tally the wins and the loses. Then, and I hope this helps, image the face of each success and tell yourself where you think they would be now if you hadn't been there. Smile at each mental photograph and then decide what you want to do; give it up or get out there again. And, I want you to know that many people are happy because of you and, along with me, admire you. Good luck with it, Moses. I suggest you stay at the shelter tonight for uninterrupted introspection."

Moses sighed deeply, "Thanks, Frank. Go home. I'll close up."

Frank didn't say another word but slipped out quietly. Moses brewed a whole pot of coffee to help him stay awake. He scratched through his hair, not knowing it was standing on end. 2 am- more coffee. Pacing, sweating with anxiety. 5 am- more coffee. He'd rest his head on the table for a few minutes then he'd pace some more; so tired. So guilty! 6 am- He lifted his head up from the table to see the breakfast crew coming in. Soon the banging of pots and pans really woke him up. His hair still stood up all over his head. He was a sight but the crew worked as though he were not there. His lips curved exhibiting a small grin.

Moses heard Jim, their driver, come in. Jim approached him as though he were there every morning, looking like a chia pet. "Morning Moses. Slumber party?"

"Yeah, the other kids were smart and went to bed." He got up and headed for the private bath room. He deserved a shower even though he was back on duty as a Homeless. The Homeless for "them". The shower for him. He had oatmeal, rounded up his cart, resolved to start a new day. Frank should have been a psychologist.

****

At the door, heading in, was Alice, a little early for her schedule. In her haste she bumped right into Moses on his way out.

"Oh, Moses, you're here. Have you seen the morning paper?" Moses nodded no. She took a deep breath and handed it to him. "Look at the picture."

How could he miss it? There he was, big as life, behind his cart; the classic homeless icon. Then the headline:

HOMELESS? HERO? CRIMINAL?

It went on to retell the Nobles' tike story; how a homeless man saved her from being hit by a speeding vehicle. Two days later is recognized by an unidentified citizen who gave details of same homeless man robbing something from St. Vincent's Church on Church St. in the early hours of July 1. Oddly enough Father Rakoczy reported candlesticks stolen from the church were mysteriously returned during the night following their disappearance. Police investigating a drowning at the Canal Street docks reported that the homeless man above was on the scene. He told police he dived in to save the boy but was unable to pull the boy to safety. Police are asking if anyone sees this homeless man to call Police Headquarters at 555-3821.

"They must have photographed me yesterday. The press were there like vultures. Also TV." Moses muttered to himself.

He looked around and settled on Alice, "What do I do now?"

Frank who had come in while Moses was trying to take in all the possible scenarios. "You've got to turn yourself in."

"What about our project here?" he worried.

Frank saw Moses' dejection. "You're innocent. The project continues. This won't put you back more than a day or two. Come on, Jim and I will go with you to the ninth precinct. They know you there."

For a minute Moses looked down in thought. "You' re right. Let's go."

One thing Moses always bounces back quickly. He walked in and met up with Officer McAllen.

"Ah, Moses. You're right coming in on your own, rather than escorted in. We'll go back to this first room and work on this." McAllen led the way. "This is for questioning; if things work out in your favor, we won't hold you. A Mr. Slavinski ID-ed you, stating you left the church with the candlesticks about 1:30 am on July 1st. The details of this event are not jibing. First of all Father Rakoczy said that the candlesticks were on the altar for morning Mass at 8 am. but disappeared before the evening Mass at 7 pm. So they had to have been stolen between the Masses scheduled for that day. When did you actually take them?"

Careful Moses. "I didn't take them at any time, but I can explain."

"Okay we'd like to hear that." Another officer had entered and sat next to McAllen, across from Moses, to take notes during the questioning."

"The boy who drowned yesterday was a lad I was trying to help; he was into drugs big time."

The officers looked at each other. "A homeless helping a druggie? Come on, Moses."

Moses looked McAllen right in the eye, "You don't know anything about me, other than I am homeless. Do I lie? Do I cheat. Do I try to make things better for others?

Am I good. Do I frighten anyone? Do I care?" Moses' demeanor never changed even though he, himself was frightened. Just a case of profiling again.

"Okay, okay. What else?"

Moses continued, "The kid's street name was Slippery. His real name? I don't know. He assumed I could fence the candlesticks for him. He told me where they'd come from. I tried to talk him into returning them personally to the Reverend. He wildly nixed that idea. So I said I would return them and he tried to grab them away from me. Just then another kid rounded the corner and Slippery saw him and his face went completely white and in his eyes was terror. He ran off, disappeared instantly. That's why The Street calls him Slippery. The demon who frightened him didn't look as though he'd even seen Slippery. Now my problem-what to do with the candlesticks? I certainly didn't want to be caught with them. I had no plausible reason for having them in my possession. If I delivered them to the Reverend, how would I explain why I had them. I knew he would think I'd stolen them. So, Mr. Whoever that saw me at the church saw me when I was returning them. He must have seen me exiting the church through the window and assumed I was stealing them. And that's odd; why didn't he call the police or contact the Reverend?" Like most people he was probably afraid to get involved. The public today fears retribution, and wisely so. However, Mr. Informant didn't mind telling the press, probably liked the thought of seeing his name in the paper. "Have you guys found out who Slippery really is or his parents?"

McAllen replied, "No, but another team is gathering info as we talk. Moses, there is something about you that you haven't told us."

"Is this true confessions? We all have something nobody else knows about us. But, no, I'm just a guy down on his luck trying to survive just like everybody else." And that was the truth! "Are we done here?"

"Yeah. You can go. But don't leave town. We' re going to question Mr. Slavinski. We might need you for a line-up or more questions."

Jim and Frank were waiting for him near the desk. "How was it?"

"Not bad but I can't leave town. Where do they think I can go? This cart ain't exactly carry-on." Frank slapped him on the back and followed him out the door.

****

Back to walking the streets. Moses thought his world was a mess when he was a 9 to 5'er. Boozing to forget. The loneliness. For his kids and, yes, for Sharon. Making all the wrong choices. And then -The Project! Now he was making a mess of that as well. "Oh, God, here I am asking for help again."

He decided to go downtown. A long walk but it would do him good. Frank had sprung for a cell phone in case McAllen called. The police officer wouldn't call directly to Moses. They'd call the Shelter and Frank would call Moses. "I wasn't supposed to afford a cell, being-you know-a homeless," his sarcasm thick with distain. Downtown was bustling. Car horns, venders shouting things to eat, a cacophony recital played in many cities, but none quite as dissonant as here in his world. He passed a bistro with outside dining- round soda fountain tables and filigree chair backs-cute. Something caught his attention. He headed back and passed again as a waiter was shouting at a woman sitting at one of the tables, holding a small child who was crying. A small suitcase stood at her feet. The waiter waved his arms as he spoke to her, "You cannot take a table unless you are ordering. Sorry, you have to go!" Moses didn't think he was sorry at all. The woman quickly shifted the child up closer and reached for the suitcase at her feet.

As she descended the three steps from the patio Moses got a good look at her. She had a swollen black eye and a cut on her lip that was swollen as well, with evidence of recent bleeding. Moses offered his hand to help her down to the sidewalk. She cowered. "Don't touch me," she trembled. Moses pulled his hand back as though she were a hot potato. By the looks of her she had a habit of cowering. As she tugged her child higher on her shoulder Moses saw bruises on her arms and if examined he was positive her whole body would be mottled black and blue.

"I won't touch you, I promise but it is obvious you need help."

"I can take care of myself! Get away from me!"

Moses shook his head back and forth, "No you can't. I can help, I promise." And he stared right into her eyes. She looked into his as well.

A man approached. "Is this man bothering you, Miss?" She never looked away, staring at Moses. "No," she said, never losing contact with Moses' eyes. The man said, "Okay then." And he continued down the street.

"As I said, you need help," Moses repeated. "I can help you."

They found a bench. Surprisingly she showed no embarrassment sitting next to a homeless man she'd just met up the street. "I guess after what she'd lived through being with a scrubby, supposedly smelly old man was the least of her concerns," thought Moses.

"Do you have someone or somewhere to go?" he asked. She shook her head no. Then she said, "At least not within a few hours of here. But I don't even have the money to call.

My sister would take us if she knew; but she lives on the west coast. Might as well be Mars."

"If I could arrange for you to stay at a shelter 'til you sort things out, would you agree to that?"

She took a long time to answer, but she really had no choice. Her mind was churning; was she doing the right thing? She'd be taking a big chance she knew; not knowing this man or his claims that he could help her. Why didn't he take care of himself if he had resources? Maybe he was an angel. Maybe he was invisible to everyone else-but, no, because that man back there had seen him. She had to look out for her baby. She had to keep her safe. But unfortunately her husband had been dangerous as well. She'd take the chance. Finally, she turned to Moses and stated firmly that there was no way she would prostitute herself or any favors of any kind.

"Good. That means you're smart and decent. My name is Moses and I assure you I just want to help. I'll take you to a shelter where they will take care of your every need until you find your family to help or, if not, they'll help you gain independence, a job, an apartment-the whole nine yards. You'll have to walk to the shelter. I'll put your suit case in my cart and walk ahead of you. If your baby is too heavy you can put her in the cart too. And if you tell me your name I'll call you that."

"My name is Laura," she stated simply. She wiped tears from her face and winced when she got too close to her lip.

****

"Alice, this is Laura and this little darlin' is Mary Beth. They need our help."

"I can see that. We have a nurse back in the infirmary. Let's have her see what needs to be done to heal those wounds. Mary Beth I bet you'd like a dolly to take care of."

Laura suggested, "There's her doll in the suitcase. I know she'll be happier with her. Usually they are inseparable." She turned to Moses, "Thank you, Moses. I owe you big time."

"Pay me with prayers. I'm almost broke."

She smiled, "I'll bet you're rich in that department."

****

Moses was slower walking this afternoon. Seeing so many people in distress usually wiped him out. And there was the candlestick drama added to his weariness. That McAllen! Oh well, it isn't a surprise that most characterized the homeless as shifty, not to be trusted. And they smelled, they stole, and sometimes they were violent. And of course people were right, except violence ranked low in their behavior, though they can be easily agitated. In defense most were just down and out; hungry and lonely. The first time Moses had encountered a homeless was just passing one on the street. Maybe his motivation actually started on Maple near the rail road overhead. He sighed and turned his cart back, heading for the shelter. Loneliness! Yes!

****

He was beginning his day heading downtown under the rays of a warm and brilliant sun. He passed the bistro where he'd met Laura. He allowed a small smile. Alice was checking on her relatives today trying to find options for Laura's new- found independence, which sounded good but few who had declared total independence discovered there was always something needed. All life's decisions and behaviors happened depending on this, depending on that. The Project was conceived on that premise. Alice found some possible options; Laura would soon have control over her own life once again. Hopefully with the help of someone who loved her or at least supported her with their approval and cheer leading.

The ring of the cell phone woke him out of his reverie. Snatching the phone, "Hello." (pause) Okay, when? (pause) Okay, thanks, Frank. Oh, by the way, is there any chance it's Meatloaf night? No. Oh, well a man can dream. After talking with McAllen this could very well be my last meal at the shelter. Sort of like a condemned man. (pause) Nah, I'm only kidding. (the joke's on me). (pause) No, I'll walk to the precinct. Wish me luck. (pause) Right." He hung up. He strolled leisurely. He had plenty of time until McAllen. "You're innocent, man." He comforted himself.

"Open the door, Moses" he directed himself. "Open it, you coward." Walk to the desk, ask for McAllen. "I have an appointment with Officer McAllen," he said to the officer at the desk. McAllen was already heading for the desk, "Ah, Moses. Just a second." He told the desk officer. "Fax these papers to NYPD. Pronto! Follow me, Moses. How you doing?"

"I'll let you know after this meeting." McAllen chuckled. "Was this his way of rubbing it in, playing 'Good Cop, Bad Cop' or was he trying to reassure me I was okay? Making assumptions, Moses; didn't you accuse him of that at our last meeting? Whata' ya' know, profiling a police officer. That could get you 30 years to life."

They sat in the same room, at the same table, as before. It could use a good cleaning. McAllen spoke, "Mr. Slavinski can't be sure he saw you or that he'd seen the candlesticks. But he did see someone that night; just not positive it was you. He doesn't know that you confessed to being there. So he's reneging his charge. That's good."

Moses just sat there nodding. "However-" McAllen again, "Father Rakoczy was sure they were stolen-BUT, since they were returned unmarred, he is not pressing charges, and he has no way of saying you were involved. That's good." It was important to Moses what Father R. thought of him.

Moses nodding less so now because he was waiting for the big BUT!

"But, we've found indications the sacristy window was the illegal entry into the church, which you've already admitted to. If you plead 'guilty' we can promise a small fine and parole for 6 months, during which time you cannot leave the area. You will be assigned a parole officer, whom you'll see a minimum of one time each month or more often if needed. Whata' ya' say?"

"Hm, I tell ya' what. I'll have to think about it."

"What?" and McAllen slumped in his chair. He stared at Moses; what was wrong with this man?

"Oh, okay, I accept." And he grinned, he'd landed a 'gotch ya' on the officer. "Payback, Officer McAllen," followed by a hardy laugh.

"You, son of a bitch!" and McAllen joined in the laughter. "If you knew what I had to go through to get this offer! Don't let me see you with even-oh, hell!" Moses started to get up. "Wait a second- another thing, Moses. Are you really going to be able to pay the fine?"

"Yep!" and he stood up, shook the officer's hand, turned, and walked down the hall without another word. Actually he swaggered. He knew McAllen was watching him.

McAllen watched, shaking his head, "Well. I'll be damned."

Without turning around a voice called back, "Probably."

****

His Parole Officer was a woman named Connie Dannon. Not unattractive, blonde hair. But in Connie's world blondes did not have more fun. Her face told it all. And her heart just wasn't into her job. Her office was a small space about the size o f a cubicle, desk, file cabinet, two chairs- hers and his, at least on Thursdays at 2:30 pm. A window with no view.

First session: She began gathering information that was already in the file spread out on her desk. She ended the session stating, "For the first month I want to see you every week. Okay, you can go."

And he did. "Can't wait for Session 2. Very stimulating.

****

Second Session:

Connie began to probe his proclivity for the Homeless Life Style.

"Are you writing a book, Connie? If you say 'yes', I say 'leave me out of it and call it a mystery.'"

"Very funny Seinfeld! Is there a reason you don't want to talk about it?"

"Yes!"

"Now you make me more curious," she coaxed. "Because I don't think you are a homeless man."

Hey, this girl may be smarter than she looks; or maybe she's bored with who she is. "Why do I have to brighten her life?" he thought. He answered himself. "Because I' m supposed to. Sorry, Lord."

"Who are you, really?"

"That my dear, is none of your business!"

"Oh, that's where you're wrong, mister! For the next, almost six months everything about you is my business," was her retort.

"How old were you when you lost your virginity?"

"What?!"

"I just thought we were playing Truth or Dare. What do I get if I tell you my story?"

"Just like a man!"

"Believe me, Honey, you've got nothing to worry about from me in that department."

"Well, gosh, thanks for the compliment!" She stood up signaling his dismissal.

"You know, you're right. I'm sorry. That was plain mean and uncalled for. Seriously, I'm trying to make a better man of myself. I guess I have a lot to work on in that department." And he hung his head, extremely embarrassed. "I hurt you. I'm so sorry."

She didn't know how to react to his sincerity. Or his pretentious ego.

"Let's call it a day. See you next week."

Moses left annoyed with himself. He'd failed in his resolve, made before all this. He wanted to be a better person. As he walked to the over-pass he asked forgiveness and received it. He knew that when you are sorry, you're always forgiven by the Lord. He hoped Connie did too.

It was a warm and humid night; adding to his inability to fall asleep.

****

Session 3: It began in embarrassment for both Connie and Moses.

She asked, "What do you want to talk about?" She tapped her pencil on the desk as she looked him in the eye. She wasn't about to let him know just how badly he'd hurt her.

Moses looked down. Hung h is head. "I don't know. Ask me some questions."

She leaned back in her chair. It rolled a little but she stopped it, without having to think about it, a habit. "Tell me about yourself. Start where ever you'd like."

"Is everything within these walls confidential?"

"Of course." She moved her hips in the chair to make herself more comfortable.

Strangely he wanted to tell so he could hear it all again. Things seemed more real when you said them out loud. He felt he needed to.

He started with the break-up of his marriage.

He talked about how he had contributed to it; the booze, the infidelity, the abusive arguments. How, his new investment in faith had taught him to make amends, not only to family but to Christ. Connie squirmed a little. She'd heard 'I'm in the Lord now' many times with parolees and this might be the first time she's believed it. He went on and explained The Project. That cleared up some of the questions she had about him.

She was a good listener, he'd give her that. This parole thing wasn't what he'd thought it would be. She never checked on his habits, his where-a-bouts, was he keeping his nose clean. Things like that. And he'd really opened up to her. No one had accomplished that, not even his staff, until now.

"This is all confidential-right?" he asked again. She nodded affirmatively.

"Good, because I'm not ready to make it public; I may never be."

"This was a good session. And, FYI, my reports are mostly complimentary."

She smiled. She looked pensive. Something was on her mind.

"How come you don't ask about my comings and goings; no booze, no drugs, illegal behaviors and things like that?"

"Oh, I know you're staying legal. Quickly she changed the subject.

Connie was closing the session, "You need to know I'm taking a pass for the next two weeks. I'll call the shelter to set up the next meeting. You don't have a cell phone?"

"No, can't afford one, right?" Another lie.

"Oh, yes, of course. And, Moses, it's amazing what you're doing."

"Trying to do."

****

Now that he was alone he wondered if he shouldn't have told Connie his story. Oh, well, it had helped to put it all out there. Probably the safest way if he had to tell it. Connie showed no prejudice, as some do when you speak of your religious persuasion. "I'm free from meetings at least." He felt like a kid in school with a day off, maybe Columbus Day. "In 14 hundred and 92 Columbus sailed the ocean blue. Too bad I can't remember the tune. But then again it's probably just as well, with my voice! He felt good again.

Alice called from the shelter, "You have mail here. I'll have Frank hold it for you. Okay? Will you be here for supper?"

He answered it with his unaffordable cell phone. Don't tell Connie.

"Meatloaf?" he begged.

"No, sorry, but goulash?" Next best!

"I'm on my way!" Actually it had been a good day all the way around.

A letter. From a good buddy of his, Ace, living in upstate New York. They'd served four years together in the military. Ace was very excited. He'd just heard he would be a mentor in a group home. His clients were lower level functioning men who, if trained, could become more independent. Ace would teach them how to launder and iron their clothes. How to cook meals, yard work, small maintenance tasks. It was their home and they had to keep it up, as any home-owner would. It wasn't a facility home; it was an unattached home on a residential street. Though at first neighbors were against these 'men' living next door, the powers that be convinced them that only those considered harmless were placed. The only distinction was that they were mildly retarded. Two actually had jobs; a dish-washer and carryout for a local grocery store. And the city council prevailed. The men are so excited. It should be said that there would be one of two mentors living with the men 24-7. "Keep your fingers crossed, Moses," Ace sounded so excited.

During goulash Moses did some thinking. This sounded perfect for Puddle. After dinner Moses would round him up and present his case. First he'd better call Ace to see if he could help place Puddle. Moses felt that old excitement when he'd successfully provided for an otherwise destitute, or troubled, fellow man or woman. "Ace, this has got to work!" Moses thought.

His call-back to Ace took longer than Moses had thought it would. They had to catch-up on their lives. Ace knew of Moses' Project. Lots of questions both ways; lots of bragging as only Marines can do. Then Puddle.

Moses explained Puddle and the sweet person behind the whiskers, the smell and sloshy shoes. Ace explained that Puddle would have to be evaluated to determine if he could function in Ace's environment. Then Ace would have to be with him to see if he'd be compatible with the four men he'd be living with.

"Ace, how much time do you need to do all that?"

"Couple of weeks minimum. Any chance you can come and help with the evaluation? It would make Puddle more likely to buy into the move."

Moses thought to himself, "H-m-m. Connie's away for a while. I'll chance it and go with Puddle. Besides I can do what I want. Time spent with one client is just as important as days on the street, digging for those who need help and don't know where to turn. Puddle is important to me. Yes, Ace I'll come."

Ace suggested, "Let me get the ball rolling up here. I'll have to find Pud a place to live, he needs a NY address to qualify; supposed to have lived there six months, but we can get around that. I'll call you when everything's in place."

Too late to track Puddle down. Maybe he'll show up in Moses' bedroom again.

****

Puddle was a no-show during the night. Moses headed back to the shelter for oatmeal. He wished that he'd seen him and brought him to breakfast again.

After breakfast Moses strolled down to the water-front park. The big draw was a train ride for the tots. He'd sit down and watch the small ones delight in the ride around the perimeter of the park. Ah, there's a train now returning to the start of the ride. Moses grinned at the children. Then he started laughing when he saw Puddle sitting on the flat car right behind the engine. Puddle looked pleased with himself.

The conductor never chased Puddle off the ride. A great guy! Some homeless were not welcome around children and the ride Conductor made them move on. But not Puddle.

"Moses, hi," Puddle grinned. "I just ride to help keep the kids safe."

"You're a good man, Pud. I got lucky yesterday; I found some change. Let's get coffees and come back to the park to enjoy the kids riding. They might need you to ride again, to keep the kids safe. Okay?"

"Oh, they won't need me to ride some more. But coffee sounds good."

They walked, pushing their carts.

"Did you have breakfast?"

"Yeah, I' m good."

Of course he hadn't eaten. Just pride that made him lie. Moses felt bad but he didn't have money or any food in his cart. A fact of the homeless.

Moses and Puddle stayed together the whole day. Moses told Puddle all about the group home.

"Sounds nice," said Puddle.

"How about we find a way for you to go; would you be willing?

Remember it is 3 square meals, a real bed and four friends to help take care of the house."

Puddle stared down at the table top, "Gee, Mo, I don't think I'd fit."

And he shook his head. He pushed back the hair dangling over his eyes.

"Of course you'd fit. Pud, you are too smart to live in the streets."

"I ain't smart." Pud blushed and brushed away imaginary crumbs from his chest.

"Did I ever lie to you, Pud? If I say you are smart, then you are smart!

Think about it. But I gotta' go now, check a kid out, ya' know?" Moses stood up. Give Pud some time to think.

"I'll see you tomorrow. I want to hear a 'yes' from you."

Moses headed to the farmers' market. Mr. Barlow always gave him an apple - no money. He didn't go to the shelter. Too much to think about.

He called Frank, "I'll need money for a two-week stay with Ace. We'd better go by bus. So two tickets, food money (he needed to convince Puddle of the great food he'd have all the time.) We'll stay in the group home while he's being evaluated. Then I'll need some pocket money; and, Frank tell Alice I need to clean Pud up. And we'll need three or four sets of clothes. I know she'll take care of it. Anything new? (pause) You got it. Go ahead. Thanks Frank."

Next morning Moses went for oatmeal. All he'd had yesterday was the apple. But, boy, was it good! While he was brushing his teeth Ace called. Everything was 'Go'. He'd have to find Puddle. He looked all morning. No Puddle. The waterfront park. No Puddle.

He started up Main Street; ahead he saw a store owner, out on the street, reaming-out Puddle for something! Moses hurried. "What's going on here?" Moses asked.

The storeowner shouted, spittle visibly spraying the air in front of Puddle's face, "This bum stole an orange and a plum from my produce counter. He thought he was slick. So why wouldn't I watch you guys hanging around my store? Homeless scum, you always steal, but I caught him. Thief! Thief!" His arms were flying.

"Hey, Mister, your hatred is showing." Moses knew he was too combative sometimes, but, he just went crazy when he heard someone judge all kinds of things about the homeless. Being homeless didn't automatically make you least among the men of the world.

"He's a thief. I should call the cops!" and made two fists and shook them at Puddle.

"Come on, let's get out of here before he does call them!" He grabbed Puddle and pulled him down the street and around the corner. Moses took him right to the shelter for something to eat. Puddle would definitely be better off in a group home. Moses prayed Puddle would qualify.

Puddle was more attentive on a full stomach. One of the cooks came and sat down with him, making him feel more at home. After finishing his bacon and eggs, Moses joined him to talk. "Ya' know in a group home you would eat like this three times a day; plus snacks. You'd have money; you might actually have a job. You could pay when you wanted fruit, or anything, not like this morning. You'd never have to steal! Please say 'yes', Puddle. Besides I'd come see you. I need a place to vacation. Whata' ya' say?"

"I'm shy, Moses, you know that. But I'll try. Do I have to go on a bus by myself?"

"Great!" and Moses slapped Pud on the back, "way to go, man! No, I get to go on vacation and I'll feel more comfortable if you're there. I'm shy too."

"You are not." Puddle knew.

"Honest, and thanks Pud, for including me." Puddle saw the widest smile on Moses' face.

"I guess I'll let him come with me." And Puddle took a big swallow of luke warm coffee. The next couple of days were busy and exciting for Puddle.

Alice warned Moses that Puddle would have to see a foot doctor as soon as they arrived. Moses honestly looked forward to giving up his persona as a homeless for a while. And he couldn't wait to see his old buddy, Ace.

****

Puddle was nervous when Ace explained the evaluation. Ace told Moses that he'd worked with many of these people and he was certain Puddle would pass. And he did! Pud was trembling but smiling. He couldn't remember the last time he'd passed anything. Mo looked at Ace and they both grinned. Let Pud think he'd aced! When in fact he had! The speed of his placement was due to the big push for this new concept, Group Homes. They wanted to place more clients before any official considered it as an expense that could be swept off the budget. Ace and Moses, as well as many others, saw the project as really successful in promoting the dignity for all men, regardless of any misplaced prejudices. Puddle saw his qualification as success, seldom awarded his kind.

At the restaurant, in which they were celebrating, Moses received a call from the shelter. Frank told him he should come home right now.

What's wrong, Frank?"

"You've made the newspaper again."

"What? How?"

"All I will say until you get here is you've been exposed!"

"Oh, God! Not yet! We're not ready!" he choked.

"I'll catch the next plane. The hell with the roundtrip bus ticket. I'll let you know where to wire the money and how much. I'll call and let you know when I'm expected. Ask Jim to be on stand-by. Overtime of course. Bye."

****

Moses got in at 6 pm. Jim was there. They were soon on their way to the shelter. Moses looked calm but he wasn't. What was taking so long? Nerves!

The whole staff was there sitting around one of the dining tables. A newspaper was spread out at the empty space reserved for Moses.

Solemnly Moses sat, reached for the page with the picture of him. Even before he read any of the text he murmured, "Wait a minute! This is a picture of me taken while I was still working, before I'd left the job. This is very telling! They must know everything. How?"

"Read the article, Moses. It explains everything as far as we, your staff can determine. If there is more, it looks like this article knows only what we know." It read:

"Multi-millionaire, posing as homeless for over a year boasts a "Project" that aids the down-trodden. Members of his staff refused to tell us where he is. Though he is known as Moses to all but his staff, his real name is Joseph E. Adams, former CEO of World Beacon Finances. Adams left this position a multi-millionaire. According to our sources Adams chose to step down after experiencing discernment from the "Divine Lord" and to make amends for his messed- up personal life. Adams did not pursue the good life, but rather, invested himself in getting people who are down and out back to their own success point. With millions and millions it must be easier to follow a "divine" intervention. None the less we commend his generosity. Street people, interviewed, confirmed 'Moses' thought more of others than he did of himself."

The article goes on about his persona as homeless, as a hero, saving a small girl from a speeding vehicle, for criminal activities in the world of drugs (with an editorial comment on bigotry). (None of his successes or services to help others live within the system.) But why does a millionaire get involved in breaking and entering? Drugs? Should we measure a man by the fruits he bears? Well in Adams' case he bears some fruits that are honorable and others that are questionable. In his previous life there is no record of criminal activity. He was definitely a 'player' but there is no evidence of illegal activities.

Finally Moses looked up, opening conversation to include his staff. "How did this get out to the press. Surely, not one of us! "Alice sobbed.

"I know who did it. None of you," and all felt relieved.

"Who then?" several spoke at once.

"My parole officer! No wonder she had to take two weeks off. She had to troll for buyers. I wonder how much my story is worth? Well, we'll soon see."

Connie was exposed, lost her job. The Project got lots of attention. Surprisingly, financial donors came forward. Some knocked his religious commitment. Too bad. Moses had walked in joy. Especially since Phase 2 was picking their brains. A live-in complex, housing those who are down on their luck. The complex would be a beautiful building with single rooms for short stays as well as Studio apartments for Mothers who have 1 or 2 children who needed time to recuperate from the demons that had sent them there. Meals were provided for those without jobs. Also a home, called the Moses House, temporarily meeting the needs of mostly battered women ensuring their safety, helping them get on their feet again. Professional gratis resources were available. A big, big phase! God works in mysterious ways! Very exciting!

And surprisingly three men offered to take on the homeless persona to continue Moses' Phase 1; people who were happy to be fishers of men, as Moses had been.

His street friends changed his name to St. Moses. Ha Ha. Moses held a celebration under the expressway overpass. And slept in his old bedroom for the last time.

"Good morning, blossoms." the first thing his sleepy eyes saw. "You can't get better than this!" He hustled over to the rail road overpass. He hoped he wasn't too late. He grinned when he spotted, his friend, Hobo.

"Hey, St. Moses! On your kneels," he instructed his roommates. They struggled to their knees and made the sign of the cross, rather awkwardly for some of them.

Moses imitated the Pope and gestured the blessing sign over them. A lot of laughter. "I've come bearing a gift-for Hobo!"

Hobo turned abruptly and tried to look humble; but he couldn't pull it off. Not Hobo.

Moses handed him a box. Slowly Hobo opened it and let out a roaring guffaw. "What?" the men demanded.

Hobo dug into the box and throwing a handful of 'confetti matches', said, "Now I'll never lose! Thanks, St. Moses. Wanna' have a game?"

Moses shook his head, 'No'. He had work to do. "If any of you fella's ever need help, come right to me. No questions asked." He promised them.

****

Now it was time to talk to his best friend, JC. He entered St. Vincent's. He hurried to the cross, knelt and gave thanks for all the Lord had bestowed upon him and his Project. He needed help with Phase 2 but right now he needed help with his personal life. He missed Sharon and his kids. "Help me, Lord, to make amends for the way I treated them so carelessly. I don't know what steps to take with them. I am still a husband and a father. No divorce papers have been served. Maybe there's still hope. If they allow me I am going to be an example and role model for them. Show me the way; I can't do it without you, Lord. I accept your decisions on these things. And please take care of Trudy, Laura, Mary Beth and Pud, even Bonkers, Coonie, and Ben. Bless Phase 2. I ask these things in the name of your Son, Jesus Christ."

He was contacted by the press for a reaction to his expose'. He said only, "Whatever we do for the least of these, we do for the Lord."

Mt 25:40
I tell you, whenever you did this
for one of the least important of
these brothers of mine,
you did for me.
"Good News Bible"

He remembered the number, dialed it and waited. "Hello?"

"Sharon? It's Joe................."

SOURCES

1. Pope Francis Speaks to Our Hearts The Word Among Us Press

2. Walking with Pope Francis 30 Days with the Encyclical, "The Light of Faith" (His first Encyclical) Twenty Third Publications

3. Killing Jesus Bill O' Reilly & Martin Dugard Henry Holt and Company, LLC

4. Word Among Us July/August 2013

5. Good News Bible William H. Sadlier, Inc.

Edwards Brothers Malloy
Oxnard, CA USA
November 25, 2014